'I'll see you to

For a moment Zo
going to lean down and kiss her, and her
senses went into overdrive. She could almost
feel his mouth on hers.

No. She was never, ever going to suffer that
mixture of pity and revulsion in another man's
eyes. That meant no kissing—because kissing
led to touching, touching led to removing
clothes, and removing clothes would reveal
the scars that nobody in London City General
knew about. The scars that meant any man
would reject her.

'See you tomorrow,' she said, slipping inside
the gateway and closing the wrought-iron gate
firmly between them. 'Thanks for seeing
me home.'

Dear Reader

I was planning my next book when three doctors leaped into my head and hijacked me! Zoe, Judith and Holly trained together, are best friends, and work together at LONDON CITY GENERAL in east London.

Zoe's the clever one, a real high-flyer who's never found love. Until she meets gorgeous Brad, on secondment to Paediatrics from California. Can she heal his broken heart—and can he help her feel less haunted by the secret she hasn't even told her best friends?

Judith's the glamorous one, who delivers babies by day and sings at hospital fundraisers at night. She falls in love with Kieran, the new maternity consultant. But after a discovery threatens to tear their love apart, can she teach him to believe in her—and in himself?

Holly's the 'prickly' one with a soft heart—but it'll take a special man to get close enough to find out! She chose the fast-paced life of the Emergency Department to help her forget her lost love. But when David walks into her life again, will it be second time lucky?

The best bit about working on a trilogy was that I didn't have to say goodbye to my characters. They made appearances in each other's stories! I loved being able to explore a hospital's community and see how different departments worked together, and I hope you enjoy life in the fast lane at LONDON CITY GENERAL as much as I did.

With love

Kate Hardy

THE DOCTOR'S
TENDER SECRET

BY
KATE HARDY

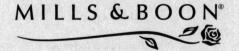

MILLS & BOON®

For Elizabeth C, with love

First published in Great Britain 2004
Paperback edition 2005
Harlequin Mills & Boon Limited,
Eton House, 18-24 Paradise Road, Richmond, Surrey TW9 1SR

© Pamela Brooks 2004

ISBN 0 263 84282 7

Set in Times Roman 10½ on 12 pt.
03-0105-48192

Printed and bound in Spain
by Litografia Rosés, S.A., Barcelona

CHAPTER ONE

BRAD HUTTON was beginning to regret his decision to oversee the paediatric assessment unit this morning. They'd had a non-stop string of cases, from suspected poisoning to asthma attacks to viruses where the GP didn't want to risk missing meningitis. The parents had all been so worried that they'd hardly heard a word he'd said and he'd had to repeat everything three times. He'd barely had time to draw breath.

The only bright spot in PAU was his registrar, Zoe Kennedy. He'd seen her around the ward over the last few days, but this was the first time he'd actually worked with her. She made him want to start humming 'Poetry in motion'—because that really was what it was like, watching her. The way she reassured the parents, scanned the notes, assessed the child and decided on the best treatment—fast, fluent, yet very thorough. And every decision he'd seen so far today had been spot on. She really knew her stuff.

Don't get too interested, a voice in his head warned him. *You're in no fit state to get involved with anyone.*

I'm not planning to get involved, he defended himself. I don't know anyone in London. A friend won't go amiss.

Just make sure that 'friends' is all it is.

It will be. Anyway, she's not my type.

She couldn't be much more than five feet three inches, whereas the girls he'd dated had always been nearer five-ten. Her hair was mouse brown and cut into a short bob, not blonde and falling almost to her waist. Her eyes were

warm and brown, not cool and blue. And beneath the
baggy long-sleeved sweater and loose jersey trousers she
wore, he had a feeling that Zoe Kennedy was all lush
curves rather than the rail-thin type he usually went for.
A pocket Venus.

Yeah, definitely Venus. She had a heart-shaped face.
Cupid's-bow lips.

And she's not Lara, the voice in his head reminded him.
*If you rush straight in to find Lara's opposite, you're not
the only one who's going to get hurt.*

'Mr Hutton?'

Then he realised that the object of his thoughts was
talking to him. 'Sorry, Dr Kennedy—Zoe, isn't it?'

She nodded.

He held out his hand. 'Brad. I prefer working on first-
name terms.'

She shook his hand and he almost flinched as a large
dose of static electricity discharged. At least, he assumed
it was static electricity. The alternative was something he
didn't want to consider right now.

'What can I do for you?'

'I'd like a second opinion on a case.'

'Sure. Though from what I've seen of you this morning,
you don't need it.'

'Um. Thanks for the compliment. But…'

Those pink spots in her cheeks were cute. She looked
young for a registrar, which meant she was clever. But
the blush at his compliment proved she'd kept at least a
trace of humility, so she'd treat her patients as human
beings, not just academic cases. 'OK. What have you
got?'

'Michael Phillips, aged twelve months. According to
the notes, he was a floppy baby. He's had problems feeding right from the start, with poor sucking and chronic

constipation; he smiled late and didn't roll over until he was eight months old. He's just starting to crawl now, but it's commando-crawling—' in other words, he lay on his stomach and propelled himself along with his arms, like a commando under a net '—and if you hold him up to stand, his reflexes aren't what you'd expect.'

'And you're thinking?' Brad prompted.

'Cerebral palsy. Probably a mixture of spastic and athetoid.'

That would account for the late development. 'What do the parents think?'

'The mum's worried sick because he's not hitting the milestones in her parenting books. The dad's in denial and saying everyone's making a fuss over nothing, his son is perfectly all right and will catch up by the time he goes to school.'

'OK. I'll come over.'

Zoe introduced him to Jenny and Dave Phillips. Brad examined little Michael. 'Tell me, does he have any problems eating?' he asked.

'Of course he does. He's a *baby*,' Dave said. 'They all dribble their food, don't they?'

'Michael doesn't like finger food,' Jenny said. 'He likes yoghurt and he'll eat purées, but he's not keen on lumps.'

'He'll grow out of it,' Dave insisted. 'You're making a fuss, Jen. He's perfectly all right.'

She shook her head. 'There's something wrong, Dave. I know it.'

'Tell her, Doc,' Dave pleaded. 'Tell her she's fussing over nothing.'

'Actually,' Brad said, 'I think she's right.'

Panic flowed in Dave Phillips's eyes. 'What's wrong with him, then?'

'We're pretty sure it's cerebral palsy,' Brad said.

'But— Are you telling me my son's...?' Dave trailed off, as if not voicing his fears would mean that it wasn't true. That it was only a bad dream. That everything was going to be all right.

Zoe squeezed his hand. 'You're both right, actually. Michael will be fine—but he'll need some help as he grows older.'

'But...cerebral palsy? He doesn't even *look* like a retard! He's bright, he points to things,' Dave burst out. 'It can't be that!'

'Cerebral palsy's a motor disorder,' Brad explained. 'It's Michael's *movements* that are affected, not his intellect.'

'A lot of children with cerebral palsy have normal or above average intelligence. There's every chance Michael will be able to go to a mainstream school rather than a special school,' Zoe added. 'The condition really varies— it can be very severe, but it can also be so mild that you hardly notice.'

Dave didn't look convinced. 'So what is cerebral palsy, then?'

'There are three types,' Brad said, 'and they all jumble the messages from the brain to the muscles. The most common form is called spastic cerebral palsy, and it's caused by an impairment in the cerebral cortex—that's the outer layer—of the brain.'

'Spastic?' Dave squeezed his eyes tightly shut. 'Oh, no. At school, we used to say...' He stopped, his face bright red with what Brad guessed was a mixture of shame and embarrassment.

Zoe must have guessed it, too, because she stepped in fast. 'The word "spastic" just means "stiff". It's referring to his muscles—they get stiff and shorten, so the child finds it hard to control his movements. It means he has to work harder than the average kid to walk or move.'

'The second sort's called athetoid cerebral palsy, and it's caused by an impairment in the basal ganglia area of the brain,' Brad said. 'It affects the child's posture and, because the muscles change from being floppy to being stiff, it causes these jerky movements and the child doesn't have any control over them. A child with athetoid CP often has speech problems because it's hard for him to control his tongue, vocal cords and breathing. He might also have problems eating and may drool. And he'll seem restless, as if he's constantly moving—as if he's only really relaxed when he's asleep.

'The third type,' he continued, 'is really rare and affects less than ten per cent of children with CP—it's called ataxic cerebral palsy, and it's caused by an impairment in the cerebellum part of the brain. This affects the child's co-ordination and balance. He often has shaky hand movements and his speech is irregular, and he'll find it hard to judge the position of things round him.'

'Which type has Michael got?' Jenny asked.

'It's very hard for us to say,' Brad admitted. 'The condition affects each child individually and he might have more than one type, in varying degrees.'

'So he's going to drool and he won't be able to walk?' Dave asked.

Zoe shook her head. 'We really can't tell at the moment. The main problem is difficulty in controlling his movements and facial expressions. He might have some learning problems—it all depends on which part of his brain has been affected. His speech might be a bit unclear, and he might find it hard to communicate—or he might have what we call a specific learning disability, say, a problem with maths or reading or drawing, if a specific part of his brain has been affected.'

Dave took a deep, shuddering breath. 'And that's it? Or can it get worse?'

'Worst-case scenario,' Brad said, 'is that he might also have a squint or hearing loss. And around a quarter to a third of children with CP have epilepsy.'

'But there's a lot we can do to help, and we can put you in touch with the local support group,' Zoe added, 'so you can talk to other parents who've been through what you're feeling right now, and they can help you.'

'Is it curable?' Jenny asked.

'There's no cure,' Brad said gently, 'but the good news is that it won't get any worse. Treatment can help to improve Michael's condition, and his disability really doesn't mean that he can't lead a full and independent life when he gets older.'

'Doesn't it?' Dave rubbed a hand across his face.

'The earlier we start treatment, the more we can help him,' Zoe said.

'So what causes it? Is it anything I did while I was pregnant?' Jenny asked.

'No, it wasn't your fault at all. The risk factors include if either of you were under twenty, he was your fifth or later child, he was a twin and the other twin died, he was very light when he was born—that's under one and a quarter kilos—or he was born more than three weeks early. Around one in four hundred babies are affected,' Brad reassured her. 'What happens is that part of the brain—the bit that controls muscles and body movements—fails to develop either before birth or in early childhood. It can be caused by a blocked blood vessel or a bleed in the brain, or a difficult labour, if he was very premature or ill after the birth, or he had an infection during early childhood, such as meningitis.'

'I can't take this in,' Jenny said. 'I knew there was something wrong. I *knew* it. But nobody would listen to me.'

'Your health visitor did,' Zoe said softly. 'She referred you to us. And sometimes it's hard to pick up—it might not show until the baby's twelve to eighteen months old. She said that he was hypotonic when he was born—that his muscles were floppy.'

'And sometimes you might find his muscles are spastic, or tight.' Brad looked at Dave. 'You might prefer the word "hypertonic". It's the same thing.'

Dave shook his head. 'I thought he was all right, that Jen was blowing everything up out of proportion and Michael was just a bit of a fussy eater. You know, not liking lumps and…well, having constipation so much.'

'They're common in children with Michael's condition,' Zoe explained. 'It might be that he's having problems chewing and swallowing. How's his sleeping?'

'Average,' Dave said.

'He only wakes up three or four times a night,' Jenny said.

Brad exchanged a glance with Zoe. By twelve months, Michael should have been sleeping through the night.

'What kind of treatment will he need?' Jenny asked.

'A physiotherapist can help you with his co-ordination—teach you exercises he can do at home,' Brad explained. 'As he gets older, a speech therapist will be able to help with speech and using language. And he'll need regular eye checks. He might not have a physical problem with his eyes, but he might find it hard to distinguish shapes.'

'That's something an occupational therapist can help

with,' Zoe said. 'The important thing is that you don't have to cope on your own—there are a lot of people who can help Michael reach his full potential.'

By the time they'd finished answering questions, made a referral to the physiotherapist and orthoptist and left the Phillipses, Zoe looked drained.

'Come on. I think we're both overdue a break. I'll shout you a coffee,' Brad said.

Zoe could feel herself blushing and was furious with herself. She really, really didn't want Brad Hutton to think she was bowled over by him. He might be tall, blond and utterly gorgeous—with those white teeth and his tan, he'd immediately been nicknamed 'surf-boy' by some of the more jealous males in the department, particularly when they found out he hailed from California—but he wasn't for her. She didn't have room in her life for a relationship. Not now, not ever. For ten years she'd kept to her decision of offering friendship, and nothing more, when it came to the opposite sex.

But this hadn't sounded like a trying-for-a-date sort of offer. It was more like a boss-rewarding-good-work sort of offer. Which meant it was perfectly safe to smile at him and say yes. 'Cheers. I think I need some caffeine,' she admitted.

Though she was still thoughtful when they were sitting in the canteen, nursing a large coffee and a muffin each.

'Penny for them?' Brad asked.

'I just hope the Phillipses will work things out,' she said. 'You know, there's a high divorce rate for parents of children with cerebral palsy, and I think Dave Phillips is going to have a lot of trouble adjusting to the idea that his son is less than perfect.'

'But they're not on their own. There are good support

groups—and you handled the situation very well. You gave him the facts, you weren't judgmental, and you gave him some hope, too.'

Pleased by the praise, Zoe met his eyes. And wished she hadn't. They were the blue of an ocean on a summer's day. The kind of eyes you could drown in.

He smiled at her. 'PAU isn't the easiest of areas. I'm glad I've got someone like you on my team—someone I can work with.'

'Thanks for the compliment, but I think you'll find the rest of the ward's the same.'

'No dragon matron?'

'No. The senior sister—Val—is more like a mother hen.' She smiled back at him. 'It's so frantic on the ward these days that you don't get time to meet people properly. Are you doing anything tonight?'

He blinked. 'Are you asking me out?'

'Um, no. Yes. Well, not me personally.'

'Thanks for the offer,' he said drily, 'but I don't need a date.'

'You're married?' She glanced automatically at his left hand. No wedding ring, no pale band of flesh hinting at the recent removal of a wedding ring either. 'But I thought you were in London on your own?'

'I *am* on my own,' he said quietly.

But there was a slight prickliness to his voice that hadn't been there before. She backtracked fast. 'I'm sorry. I wasn't trying to pick you up or anything. It's just that you're on secondment and you don't know many people around here, so I thought you might be a bit lonely.'

Lonely? She could say that again. He'd been bone-deep lonely since losing Lara. 'I'm OK.'

'Well, I'm going out with Jude and Holls tonight— they're my best friends—and I wondered if you'd like to join us. Nothing fancy, just pasta and the house red at our local Italian.'

'Thanks, but I'm fine.'

'If you change your mind, we'll be at Giovanni's from about seven tonight until they chuck us out.'

She was planning to drink until closing time? 'I hope you're on a late tomorrow.'

She didn't seem at all offended by his rudeness. Her eyes were lit with amusement and she grinned at him. 'No, I'm on an early. So after the second glass of wine I'll be on mineral water. Until we start on the ice-cream— and then it's coffee all the way. Giovanni's does the best latte in London.'

He should have guessed that, from what he'd already seen of her. Zoe was a professional. She wouldn't come on duty with a hangover. 'Right.'

'So are you busy next Wednesday night?'

She was persistent, he'd give her that. 'Why?'

'If you're not, how would you like to make some money?'

He frowned. 'You're going to a casino? Or...' Hadn't he heard someone on the ward talk about greyhound racing? 'The dogs?'

She shook her head. 'Nothing like that. It's a fundraiser for medical equipment. Jude, Holls and I do it once a month, and split the proceeds between our wards— Jude's in maternity and Holls is in Emergency. So we all benefit.'

'What's involved?'

'You can buy a ticket, for a start. Or go and flash your smile around, flutter your eyelashes and talk people into buying tickets. Unless...' She looked thoughtful. 'You're not musical, by any chance, are you?'

'I play the piano a bit,' he admitted.

Big mistake.

'Yes!' She punched the air. 'I think I've just found our guest star.'

'Hang on.' This was all going way too fast. 'I'm out of practise. I'm rusty.'

'You've got a week. You can practise on Jude's piano.'

'But…' His protest died as he realised that he had no chance of winning. Zoe would come up with an answer for any excuse he made.

She gave him that grin again. The one that put amber glints into her brown eyes. 'That's settled, then. Thanks. We'll add your name to the posters. Guest star, Brad Hutton—is that vocals as well as piano?'

'Has anyone ever told you you're a…?' He shook his head. Words failed him.

Zoe chuckled. 'My nickname on the ward's Hurricane Zoe.'

'It suits you,' he said feelingly.

'So, is it piano only, or vocals?'

He sighed. 'Both. I don't have any choice, do I?'

'You can say no.'

But that would mean letting her down. With shock, Brad realised that he didn't want to do that. He didn't want to see disappointment spill over her face. Which meant that Zoe Kennedy was the first person he'd actually responded to in nearly a year. He wasn't sure if that made him feel relieved—that he hadn't become a complete automaton, that he could still feel something—or scared. 'How many people are there?'

'It's not a huge thing, it's in the hospital social club. We sell quite a few tickets—Holly can be very, um, persuasive—but only about thirty people tend to turn up. I do the food, Holls does the tickets and Jude wows everyone with her singing.' She gave him a sidelong look. 'Perhaps you should change your mind about coming to Giovanni's tonight. You need to talk set lists with Jude and posters with Holls. Unless you want to leave the decisions with me?'

With Hurricane Zoe? He'd never heard a nickname that fitted someone so well. Heaven only knew what she'd agree to on his behalf! 'I'll be there tonight,' he said.

'Good.' She sketched a map hurriedly on the back of a paper napkin. 'This is London City General,' she said, marking a big block on the paper. 'You go out of the main entrance, turn right down this little street here, take a left, then the second right, and Giovanni's is on the corner.' She circled a smaller block. 'It's pretty easy to find. Look for the green, red and white stripy shutters.'

'Won't your boyfriends mind me joining you?'

She shook her head. 'It's just the three of us tonight. Besides, Holls and Jude are happily married to their careers.'

What about Zoe? She hadn't said she was single. She hadn't said she was attached either. Though why was he even wondering about it? He wasn't in the market for a relationship. Not now, probably not ever—it had been nearly a year now and he still felt as lost. It was one of the reasons why he'd leapt at the London secondment, to go somewhere where there were no memories to haunt him.

Zoe Kennedy wasn't for him. And the chances were she was already attached anyway.

'Good. Seven o'clock at Giovanni's, then.' She smiled at him. 'We'd better get back, or there'll be a list of patients as long as my arm!'

CHAPTER TWO

BRAD was late. When he arrived at Giovanni's, the three women were already seated at a table, drinking red wine, with a spare place laid for him.

One of Zoe's friends was tall and beautiful with creamy skin and long red hair twisted back in a knot; the other was dark and intense-looking. And then there was Zoe, shorter than both, mid-brown hair that had copper lights when the sun caught it, and a Cupid's-bow mouth with creases at the sides to show how often she smiled.

He wasn't going to let his thoughts drift in *that* direction. He had nothing to offer her anyway. He was about to walk out of the door, planning to make some excuse in the morning when he had to face Zoe and she asked him why he'd stood them up, when she spotted him and waved.

No way could he back out now.

Fixing a smile on his face, he went over to join them. Zoe performed quick introductions. The redhead was Judith, an obstetrician, and the brunette was Holly, an emergency specialist. They'd been best friends since their first day of med school, over ten years before.

'Zo tells us you're at London City General on second-ment from California. How are you enjoying it?' Judith asked.

'It's…different.' And, more importantly, London was somewhere that didn't remind him of Lara. Even though they'd planned years before to snatch some time in

17

London together, it had never quite worked out that way. It was free of memories.

'Do you miss it? California, I mean?' Holly asked.

Only the bit that he could never have again. Not that he was going to burden them with his problems. 'I miss the weather,' he said, trying to keep things light. 'I didn't realise it was quite this cold over here.'

'It's not *that* cold. Don't be such a wimp,' Zoe said.

Judith chuckled. 'Here, have a glass of wine.' She poured a glass for him. 'Ignore our Zo. She's mad enough to go paddling in November.'

'A walk on the beach in winter is good for you. It blows the cobwebs out,' Zoe defended herself, laughing.

'Her aunt's got a cottage on the Norfolk coast, and Zo's dragged us out there before now in the middle of winter for a picnic on the beach,' Holly said, shivering.

'When it was sunny?' Brad guessed.

'Er…no. It wasn't actually raining, but it wasn't far off.' Judith raised an eyebrow. 'I suppose we were just lucky it was a flask of her home-made soup in the picnic basket and not a Thermos of ice-cream.'

So Zoe had a kooky streak. She went paddling in the North Sea in November. Had beach picnics in the middle of winter. Loved ice-cream. And could cook.

'Anyway, we're treating you to dinner tonight,' Zoe announced. 'Seeing as I practically bullied you into singing with Jude next week, it's the least we can do.'

She had that determined look on her face again. Brad decided it was easier not to argue. 'Thank you. So how long have you been doing these fund-raisers?'

'The Wednesday night music club? Nearly a year,' Judith said. 'It was Zo's idea. Paeds needed some equipment and the finance lot wouldn't cough up.'

'So she did a promise auction to raise the funds,' Holly said.

'She talked me into promising to sing for one night at London City General Social Club,' Judith explained, 'and somehow it's grown into this monthly thing.'

'I think I mentioned that we split the proceeds between Paeds, the maternity unit and the emergency department,' Zoe said. 'I'll go and sort some more wine while you three talk set lists and promotional stuff. Red OK with everyone?'

By the end of the evening, Brad was surprised to find that he was enjoying himself. A lot. It was the first evening in nearly a year when he hadn't spent every single second thinking of Lara. Zoe might be a whirlwind, but she had a good heart, and she'd even given him another chance to back out of the Wednesday night fund-raiser without losing face—not that he'd taken her up on it. He still didn't want to disappoint her.

Between the three of them, they'd brought him completely out of his shell—to the point where he was even sharing scurrilous anecdotes with them and swapping med school jokes. He'd thought he'd never be able to smile again, let alone laugh. But there was something about Zoe, something warm and friendly and kind and—

Stop right there, he told himself. You're not getting involved.

'Right. I'm on an early tomorrow, so I'm going to leave you party animals to it,' Zoe announced after her third latte.

Judith glanced at her watch. 'I didn't realise it was that late! I'd better be making tracks, too.'

'And me,' Holly said. 'I've got a paper I'm supposed to be finishing.'

'I'll see you home,' Brad said, and they all started laughing. 'What?' he asked, mystified.

'It's very gentlemanly of you, and we appreciate the offer. But, apart from the fact that we've all lived around here since we were students and know the area like the backs of our hands, Holl's my next-door neighbour. So we're fine walking each other home,' Judith told him, tucking her hand into the crook of Holly's elbow.

'I'm fine, too,' Zoe put in swiftly.

'You live in the same road?' Brad asked.

'Er, no. In the opposite direction,' she admitted.

'Then how do I put it? Let me see you home safely, or I might pick up a virus from one of our patients next Wednesday afternoon which stops me singing or playing the piano,' Brad said.

'Do as the man says, Zo,' Holly directed. 'Or you'll have to take his place next week and sing with Jude.'

'They'd probably pay us even more for me *not* to sing,' Zoe teased, but it was obvious she realised she was beaten and she gave in with good grace. She hugged the others goodbye and then she was walking down the narrow side streets with Brad.

'They're nice, your friends,' Brad said.

'The best,' Zoe said feelingly. 'Look, I bulldozed you a bit about the fund-raiser.'

'A bit?'

'A lot. What I'm saying is, if you'd rather not, I do understand.'

'No, I'll do it. It sounds like fun.'

'It is,' Zoe said.

They lapsed into silence, but it was companionable rather than awkward. When they reached Zoe's terrace, they stopped outside the gate.

'I'd ask you in for coffee,' Zoe said, 'but...'

'The boyfriend wouldn't like it?' Brad guessed.

'Something like that.' If she had a boyfriend. Not that she wanted one. She was perfectly happy with her career as a paediatrician.

'Then I'll see you tomorrow.'

For a moment, she thought that he was going to lean down and kiss her, and her senses went into overdrive. She could almost feel his mouth on hers. Soft, a little unsure at first, and then coaxing as she responded. And then—

What's this? You're… Oh, God. I'm sorry, Zoe. I can't do this…

The words echoed in her mind, the words that had haunted her for ten years. The words that brought her back to the real world every time she thought that maybe it was time to drop her self-imposed ban on a relationship.

Damaged goods.

No. She was never, ever going to suffer that mixture of pity and revulsion in another man's eyes. That meant no kissing—because kissing led to touching, touching led to removing clothes, and removing clothes would reveal the scars that nobody in London City General knew about, not even Holly and Judith. The scars Zoe kept well out of sight beneath long-sleeved, high-necked tops, or shirts that didn't even have a hint of sheerness in their fabric. The scars that meant any man would reject her.

'See you tomorrow,' she said, slipping inside the gateway and closing the wrought-iron gate firmly between them. 'Thanks for seeing me home.'

If Brad had noticed Zoe clamming up on him, he didn't make an issue of it, to her relief. He was completely normal with her at work over the next couple of days, treating her as a valued colleague. A doctor, rather than a woman:

which was just the way she wanted it. That was who she was. Dr Zoe Kennedy, paediatrician. Everyone's friend. And nobody's lover.

'Can I borrow you for a minute, Zoe?'

'Sure.'

'I've got a case of suspected osteomyelitis,' he said. 'Little boy name of Andy Solomon. Aged six, soccer fanatic. Anyway, a couple of days ago he turned down a game of soccer in the park with his pals. His mum thought it was a bit strange—thought maybe he'd bruised himself as he'd been limping and his knee looked a bit swollen. That night, he developed a really high temperature. He's flushed, restless—and she said the pain's been getting worse. The GP referred him to us for an X-ray, bone scan and blood tests.'

'Have you examined him?' Zoe asked.

Brad nodded. 'He's still got a fever—even though his mum's been giving him infant paracetamol—the swelling and redness is obvious, it feels warm around the area and it's clearly tender because he shielded his leg when I tried to palpate it.'

'So you want blood tests—white blood cell count, erythrocyte sedimentation rate and C-reactive proteins. If it's been going on for a few days…X-rays and an MRI scan? And a culture so we can see what's causing it? Though in eighty per cent of cases it'll be *Staph aureus*.'

'You know your stuff.' He gave her a quick smile that had her knees turning to jelly, despite her resolution not to let herself go all weak at the knees over him. 'Can you start him on IV antibiotics?'

'Broad spectrum until we've got a definite fix on the bacterium, then penicillinase-resistant synthetic penicillin and aminoglycoside if it's *Staph aureus*?' she suggested.

'Perfect.'

'OK. I'll sort him out and let you know when the results are back. Have you and Jude sorted out your set list for next week yet?'

'Nearly. Any requests?'

No way. Having a man singing to her—especially one as gorgeous as Brad—would be way too dangerous for her peace of mind. He'd probably thought she'd been fishing, so she'd better make it clear. 'Not really. I like all sorts of music,' she said. 'Sing whatever you like, as long as you make us a pile of money.'

'Sure. Have you sorted out the menu yet?'

'Nearly. Any requests?' The words were out before she could stop them. Rats. She was definitely letting him get to her. She should have told him yes and stopped there.

'Now you come to mention it… Yes. Proper American brownies. I haven't tasted one since I've been in England,' he said.

That brought up all kinds of suggestive thoughts. Like sitting on the edge of his desk while he reclined in his chair, his mouth open, while she fed him tiny bites of brownie. In between kisses.

Absolutely not. They were colleagues, they might become friends, but they could never be anything else. 'I'll see what I can do.' Right now, she needed to escape. And he'd given her the perfect excuse. 'I'd better go and see Andy Solomon.'

She found little Andy and settled him into his bed.

'I don't know where this has all come from,' his mother said. 'He was fine. Then suddenly, bang, he doesn't want to get up for school, doesn't want to take his football in with him, he's off his food…'

'Has he had any illness recently—a cold, a runny nose, a sore throat?' Zoe asked. Osteomyelitis was a bacterial bone infection and the bacteria could come from a nose or throat infection as well as through a puncture wound.

'Nothing.' Mrs Solomon shook her head. 'He's never ill. Yeah, he gets all the usual bumps and scrapes any other six-year-old boy has. Climbing trees, falling over in the playground, that sort of thing.'

'Any scrapes recently?'

'A month or so back. But, well, all his vaccinations are up to date. I made sure he had his tetanus and that. And grazed knees don't make you this unwell, do they?'

'They can do, if bacteria get in the wound,' Zoe said. 'Sometimes the bacteria can lie dormant for weeks and something just sets it off.'

'I've always cleaned him up properly,' Mrs Solomon said, lifting her chin. 'He has a bath every night, too.'

'It's nothing to do with hygiene,' Zoe reassured her.

'So you think it's this osteo-whatever, too?'

'Osteomyelitis. It's a bone infection. What we're going to do is some tests to find out what's causing it and how much Andy's bone has been infected. Once we know that, we'll know how to treat it properly. I've got him booked in for an X-ray, and I'll need to take some blood and a little sample of the tissue round the bone.' She smiled at her small patient. 'Do you like planes?'

'Yeah,' the little boy replied, sounding completely unenthusiastic.

'Come on, Andy. You know you love going down the airport with your dad,' Mrs Solomon prompted.

'Well, I've got some special plane stickers. Holographic ones,' Zoe said. 'And I only give them to my bravest patients. So if you can stay really, really still for me while I do this sample and start the antibiotics—look at your mum or me, not at my hands—you'll get a sticker. Deal?'

'Deal,' the little boy replied seriously.

'OK. Here we go, then. Now, tell me, who's going to be top of the Premier League this year?'

'Manchester United!' the little boy said. 'They're my team. Dad's going to take me to see them.' His voice wobbled. 'Ow, that hurts.'

'I know, sweetheart, but it's only for a little while and I'm doing it so I can make you better,' Zoe soothed. 'So who's your favourite player?'

She managed to keep him talking about football until she'd finished capping her sample and put the line in for the antibiotics. Then she smiled at the little boy and took her sheet of stickers out of her pocket. 'You were so brave, I think I'll let you choose your own,' she said.

'That one. It's not like the one my dad flies, but it's cool,' Andy said. Then remembered his manners. 'Thank you.'

'My pleasure. I'm going to get this off to the lab now, so they can test it for me.' She looked at Mrs Solomon. 'I'll be back to see you later on. In the meantime, if you need anything, buzz one of the nurses. June's going to be looking after you—she's really nice and very experienced, so she'll be able to answer a lot of your questions. I'll make sure she brings you a card for the coffee-machine and tells you where everything is.' She ruffled Andy's hair. 'And then you can choose what you're having for lunch.'

'Cool,' Andy said.

Later that day, Zoe rapped on Brad's office door.

'Come in,' he said.

'Andy's bloods are back. His white blood cell count is completely normal.'

'Well, it doesn't always alter in osteomyelitis.'

She nodded. 'But his ESR—' the erythrocyte sedimentation rate '—is elevated, and so is his C-reactive protein. That's pretty suggestive. I've had a look at his X-ray, too.'

'You got the films back already?'

She grinned at his surprise. 'I'm good at nagging. Anyway, there's haziness and a rounded shadow pretty much where you'd expect it. I'd say it's osteomyelitis in the upper tibia.'

He took the proffered films and checked them on the light-box. 'Spot on, Dr Kennedy. Looks like there's some loss of bone density there, too, so we need to keep a close eye on it. What about the biopsy?'

'It'll be another couple of days before the culture's ready, but it's bound to be *Staph aureus*. It usually is.'

He sighed. 'Right. Now to explain it all to Andy's mum.'

'Want me to come with you?'

Why on *earth* had she said that? He was the consultant—he didn't need anyone with him to hold his hand and help him with a patient's parents. 'Um, just that I got talking to her earlier. A friendly face, and all that. And…' No, she was only digging a deeper hole for herself.

But instead of the sarcastic comment she was expecting—and which she knew she deserved—he merely said, 'Thanks.'

And then she made another mistake. She looked into his eyes. They were mesmerising: that was the only word to describe them. Why else would she feel her lips parting slightly? Why else would they be so dry that she needed to lick them? Why else would she suddenly start imagining his face closer and closer to hers, his mouth growing nearer and nearer until it finally touched hers, first with gentle kisses, and then coaxing a response from her until…?

But it wasn't going to happen. No matter how attractive she found Brad, she wasn't making any exceptions to her rule.

Damaged goods. Remember that, she told herself.

Somehow she managed to get her thoughts together and followed him through to the bay to Andy Solomon's bed. Andy was asleep and his mother was sitting there, holding his hand and looking desperately worried.

'We've had the results of the tests back, Mrs Solomon. It's osteomyelitis, as we suspected. What that means is that the bone's infected and inflamed.' Brad drew a quick diagram to show her what he meant. 'The bones are covered with a membrane which contains the nerve endings, plus lots of small blood vessels that deliver the nutrients to the bone. Pus collects beneath it and forms an abscess which makes it stretch—that's why Andy says it hurts. It also squashes the blood vessels—and because the bone isn't getting the nutrients it needs, it starts to die off.'

'So is he going to lose his leg?' Mrs Solomon asked, aghast.

'Not at all. In the days before antibiotics, it killed a quarter of people who got it, and crippled another quarter. Nowadays, the antibiotics do the hard work for us and he'll recover perfectly—especially as you brought him in so quickly.'

'Jim always says I make a fuss,' Mrs Solomon said wryly. 'But it's hard, with him being a pilot and away so much—half the time it feels like I'm a single mum. There's only me to make the decisions.'

'You made the right one here,' Brad reassured her.

'But how did it happen?' she asked.

'Acute haematogenous osteomyelitis is caused by a bacterium which entered Andy's body—maybe through a throat infection, maybe through a graze—and lay dormant for a while before it seeded in the bone. The most common site is in the long growing bones, in the arms or legs—it affects the growing area, at the ends. It's twice as common in boys than in girls,' Brad explained. 'The infection can spread to the soft tissues and joints, and if the bone tissues die you need surgery to get rid of the dead tissue so the bone can regrow itself.'

'So he's not going to be lame or anything?' Mrs Solomon asked.

'No. What we're doing now is giving him antibiotics which will penetrate the bone. It's a broad spectrum at the moment because it takes a couple of days to grow the bacterium from the sample I took,' Zoe explained. 'Once we know what it is, we might need to change the antibiotics, and he'll need to stay in for a couple of weeks so we can keep an eye on him. If he needs surgery, we'll be able to pack the hole in his bones to help him grow new bone tissue. In the meantime, we're giving him a splint to hold his leg still.'

'He'll be on antibiotics for the next couple of months,' Brad continued. 'He can probably go home in a couple of weeks and take them in a tablet form, but he has to keep taking them until we're happy with his blood count and his X-rays. Once the bone's healed, it should continue to grow properly, but we'll have him in for regular check-ups to keep an eye on it.'

'He might need building up for a few months afterwards, too,' Zoe added. She grinned. 'Which he'll take as an excuse for scoffing all the chocolate he can get his hands on!'

'Who needs an excuse?' Brad teased.

'Don't listen to him. He's addicted to chocolate brownies,' Zoe said.

'You two must have worked together for a long time,' Mrs Solomon commented. 'You're so in tune.'

Not that long. A handful of days, Brad thought. And the worst thing was, he couldn't remember being this in tune with anyone else, ever. Even Lara. Which made him feel even more guilty. He really shouldn't be thinking about another woman so soon after Lara. Particularly one who was committed elsewhere—Zoe had made that clear when he'd walked her home. The lack of a ring on her left hand meant nothing: she didn't need a wedding ring or even an engagement ring to be deeply in love.

Though he couldn't help wondering what sort of man Zoe would choose. The tall, dark, Celtic type, he guessed, with clear skin and blue eyes. Someone laid-back. Or would he be more like her, always on the go, always coming up with new schemes? Somehow he couldn't imagine Zoe putting up with someone wishy-washy, a man who never made decisions. She was too much of a whirlwind, she'd lose patience.

He shook himself. It wasn't any of his business anyway. He wasn't a relationship-breaker. Zoe was off limits and she was staying that way. She had to. For his sanity's sake.

CHAPTER THREE

THE following Wednesday, Brad spotted his name on the staff notice-board. On a poster for Judith's Wednesday Night Music Club, billing him as the 'star guest'. And in bright pink highlighter pen, the words 'Sold Out' were printed neatly across the poster.

He went to find Zoe. 'How many people are going to be there tonight?' he asked suspiciously.

'I'm not sure. People often give Holly the money for a ticket or the raffle, but don't actually come to the show.'

'How many tickets have you sold?'

At least she had the grace to blush. 'A hundred and fifty. That's the maximum we can have in the social club because of the fire regulations.' She looked at him in dismay. 'Please, don't tell me you're having second thoughts. Not now.'

Second? He was having third—and fourth! 'It's been a while since I played in public.' He coughed. 'And you said there were usually only about thirty people there.' There was a big difference between thirty and a hundred and fifty. Like five times as many.

'They probably won't all come.'

'But you've sold more tickets than usual?'

'Yes. Probably because of you—the curiosity factor,' Zoe admitted. 'But it's for a good cause. It nets us tons of money for the wards. The social club does the bar and gives us half the profits for the night. And...' She waved a paper bag at him. 'Sample. As promised.'

'I hope,' Brad said through gritted teeth, 'that bag contains chocolate brownies. In the plural.'

'It does. Look, you'll be fine. Just pretend you're playing to an audience of one.'

He wished she hadn't said that. Because right now he could imagine playing the piano to Zoe. By candlelight, or maybe moonlight. Just the two of them. Something soft and romantic and seductive.

No. Cool, calm and sensible, he reminded himself. 'An audience of one.' Damn. His voice was cracking. He hoped she hadn't noticed. Or, if she had, that she'd put it down to nerves—he didn't want her knowing how much of an effect she had on him. It would make her run a mile, and he wouldn't blame her.

'It's a psychological technique. Jude uses it, too,' Zoe said helpfully. 'It usually works well. Or imagine all the people in the front row are naked or something.'

Naked. Did she *have* to use that word? Because if she was in the front row tonight... He dragged his thoughts back and grabbed the mental equivalent of a bucket of cold water. 'Is your boyfriend helping out tonight?'

'Mmm,' Zoe mumbled. 'Anyway, here are your brownies. I'll, um, catch you later.'

She avoided him for the rest of the morning, though he seemed to keep coming across her wake, such as another sticker for Andy Solomon, earned for letting her take a blood sample without fuss, or the 'bravery certificates' she drew for a couple of other patients. He couldn't find her in the afternoon, and discovered that she'd taken a half-day—presumably to finish cooking for the social evening.

The next thing he knew, he was sitting on the stage behind the piano, running sound checks with Judith. Zoe was somewhere around—he could feel it in his bones—but she seemed to be avoiding him. Or maybe he was just being paranoid. He hadn't done anything to drive her away. Hadn't touched her, hadn't kissed her.

Though he'd wanted to. Lord, how he'd wanted to.

And he really shouldn't want. It wasn't fair on either of them.

'Are you OK?' Judith asked.

'Just a bit nervous,' he admitted.

'You'll be fine. Just imagine you're singing to an audience of one. I usually sing to Holls or Zo, like I did when we shared a flat as students,' Judith said.

They ran through a couple of songs. And the next thing he knew, the room was filling up with people. He couldn't see Zoe anywhere. Though the hairs on the back of his neck told him that she was definitely around.

By the third song, Brad had forgotten his nerves. He joined Judith in a version of 'American Pie' that had everyone tapping their feet and singing along. From there, they launched into a couple of blues standards. And then someone requested 'Fever'.

He sang along with Judith, but he couldn't help scanning the crowd for one person. The one he finally saw right at the back of the room. The one who really did give him a fever, even though she shouldn't.

He'd said he could sing a bit. Not that he had a voice that could melt your bones, Zoe thought. Deep and warm and soulful, blending perfectly with Judith's husky jazz-singer tones. Just for a moment, she imagined herself as his audience of one. Imagined him singing just for her. Singing words of love.

She turned away and concentrated on doing the food. In the background, organising things. Just what she did best.

But then she froze as Brad launched into Van Morrison's 'Brown-Eyed Girl'. Judith may have been singing along with him, but she could only hear his voice. Singing about a girl with brown eyes. Brown eyes, like her own.

Worse still, someone requested another Van Morrison song, slowing the mood down with 'Have I Told You Lately?'.

And she was lost.

Somehow—she wasn't even aware of moving—she worked her way to the front of the crowd. Met Brad's eyes over the top of the piano as he crooned the words.

Insane. He must be going completely insane. Zoe Kennedy was off limits. And here he was, singing one of the most romantic songs ever written. To her. And he really was singing just to her, not to the appreciative crowd.

She must know it. She had to know it. Why else would she be standing there at the front, smiling back at him?

Unless she was smiling at the boyfriend.

Brad scanned the room. He couldn't see anyone who looked as though he was with Zoe. Nobody with his arm round her waist, holding her against him and humming those same words to her, a tribute to a woman who could wipe away his sadness and fill his heart with love. Zoe was standing there alone, looking at him. And Brad was looking right back at her.

Was Zoe the one who could wipe away *his* sadness?

It was stupid to feel jealous, Zoe told herself crossly. Jude was only singing with Brad to raise money. So why was she wishing that she was the one up on stage with him instead of her best friend? Why was she wishing that Brad and Jude didn't look quite so good together? Why was she panicking that Jude might decide that her career wasn't enough after all, and Brad was what she wanted? And that Brad would, of course, fall for the most gorgeous woman in the hospital, five feet eleven with legs up to her armpits, long red hair, clear skin and blue eyes, who sang like an angel and had a lot more in common with him than Zoe did?

This really, really wasn't good. Zoe never panicked about men. Ever. She didn't have a love life to upset her equilibrium; she didn't do more than smile with her friends about the latest heart-throb actor or singer or sports star. So why was she feeling like this about Brad Hutton?

Then the music changed tempo again as someone requested something upbeat, fun and frothy. Relieved that she hadn't quite made a fool of herself, Zoe escaped back to her table duties, topping up the empty platters from the boxes she'd stored in the kitchen cooler.

When the evening was over and the crowds had gone, Zoe started clearing up. A voice said beside her, 'Anything I can do?' and she dropped the stainless-steel dishes she was holding.

Lucky they weren't glass, she thought as they clattered loudly onto the table.

'Sorry. I didn't mean to startle you,' Brad said.

'No. I was miles away. Just thinking about how well it went tonight.'

'Did you make a lot?'

'Dunno. Ask Holly—she's doing the tally.'

'Didn't your boyfriend stick around to help?'

Zoe felt her cheeks grow hot. 'He couldn't make it tonight,' she mumbled. Well, of course her boyfriend hadn't been able to make it. He didn't exist!

'Do you want a hand with the washing-up?'

'I'm fine. I've got a deal with the kitchen staff,' she said. 'They let me use the dishwasher in exchange for cake.'

'You've really got a network here, haven't you?' he asked admiringly.

She shrugged. 'I'm just part of the hospital. A small part.'

A big part, he'd say. Hurricane Zoe might be bossy, but her heart was solid gold and he hadn't met a single person who didn't adore her. Which was yet another reason why he should stay away from her. If he so much as laid a finger on her, most of London City General would be baying for his blood, as the man who'd wrecked her relationship and broken her heart.

And he'd hate himself just as much, for hurting her. For her sake, he had to stay away.

'What do you want me to do?' he asked.

She shook her head. 'You've done your bit. Look, I saved some food for you and Jude. You must be hungry. Go and eat.'

'OK, boss,' he said, and wandered over to join Judith and Holly. 'How did we do?' he asked Holly.

'Brilliantly.' Holly told him the total and his jaw dropped.

'We made all that in one night?'

'Donations, ticket sales and half the bar profits. Thanks to you.'

'Hey. I'm not the one who set it up.'

'No, but you were a good enough sport to let Zo persuade you into singing with Jude. And it takes a lot of nerve to stand up on stage and do what you did. I couldn't do it.'

'Here. Have one of Zo's brownies,' Judith offered. 'Before I scoff them all. They're seriously good.'

Brad decided not to admit he'd already had three—and that Zoe had brought them to the ward that morning, especially for him.

That she'd made them on his request.

'Thanks.' He took a brownie. 'Mmm, you're right, these are really good.'

'Yet another of Zo's talents. She's good at everything,' Judith said.

'Except singing,' Holly corrected with a grin. 'She's got a tin ear. Worse than mine!'

Brad didn't care. He didn't want Zoe to sing to him anyway. There were other, much more pleasurable things he could imagine her sweet mouth doing.

'Is Zoe's boyfriend a doctor?' he asked, as casually as he could.

'Zoe's boyfriend?' Judith asked, sounding mystified.

'Mmm. The guy she hangs round with.' He shouldn't be asking. It was none of his business. But he couldn't help wanting to know—wanting to be sure that the man Zoe loved deserved her. Her best friends would know that, wouldn't they? 'She said he couldn't make it tonight—that he usually helps. Did he get called back to his ward or something?'

He saw the glance pass between Judith and Holly, and frowned. 'What am I missing?' Oh, no. Please. Don't let her have fallen for a selfish jerk who resented the time she spent on other people and left her to do everything on her own.

'Um, nothing,' Judith said, a little too brightly.

'You're interested in our Zoe, aren't you?' Holly asked.

Brad swallowed. Was it that obvious? 'What makes you think that?' he prevaricated.

'Because you were singing to her tonight,' Judith said.

Brad rubbed his hand across his face. Hell. It really *was* that obvious. Judith and Holly knew, too. 'I…um…'

As if she'd guessed his worries, Holly added, 'Don't worry. No one else noticed. We only did because— *Ow.*' She rubbed her ankle.

'Because what?' Brad asked. Had Zoe said something to them about him?

'Because we're her best friends,' Judith said.

Maybe he'd got it wrong. He backtracked, fast. 'Look, I'm not going to hurt her. I promise. I know she's in love with this boyfriend of hers and I'm not going to interfere.'

'For a consultant,' Holly said, 'you're not very bright, are you?'

Brad frowned again. 'How do you mean?'

'Zoe doesn't *have* a boyfriend,' Judith told him quietly.

This didn't make sense. Not at all. 'But why would she say she did, when she doesn't?'

'Because she—' Holly stopped and glared at Judith.

Whatever she'd been about to say, Brad thought, Judith had guessed and hadn't wanted Holly to tell him. She'd obviously kicked Holly under the table to stop her talking. 'What?' he pressed.

Holly shrugged. 'Maybe she thinks having a relationship means that no one will take her seriously in her career.'

'So she's single.'

'Yes,' Judith confirmed.

'And you think she'd be interested in me? If I…?' Brad's thoughts were whirling. Zoe wasn't seeing anyone else. Zoe wasn't off limits. They could…

'Just talk to her,' Holly said.

*   *   *

Talk to her. *Talk to her.* Well, that was easier said than done, Brad thought two days later. Zoe refused point-blank to have a personal conversation with him. She'd spend any amount of time with him discussing patients or treatments or clinical protocol, but the minute he tried to switch the conversation onto a more personal level, she switched it right back.

'Are you busy tonight?' he asked her.

Zoe picked up a file. 'I was wondering about PKU,' she said.

'PKU?'

'Phenylketonuria. A genetic enzyme deficiency.'

He smiled. 'I know what PKU is.'

'I had a patient today. A little girl, fifteen months old. She was very fair, though both her parents were dark. She has eczema. And she's not talking much—she's hardly babbling. She pushes other children away if they go anywhere near her. And I was wondering if the developmental delay could be a side-effect of PKU.'

'I thought all newborns were screened here for PKU?'

'They are. Well, they're supposed to be. You know some always slip through the net,' Zoe said.

'Hmm. Did she smell a bit odd—a bit like mice?'

Zoe nodded. 'And the fairness, given her parents' colouring—I wondered if it was tyrosine deficiency.' With PKU, the body didn't have enough phenylalanine hydroxylase so it could only convert some of the amino acid phenylalanine into tyrosine. Phenylalanine then built up in the blood and brain, and could cause severe damage.

'So what's the plan?'

'I did a blood sample to check her plasma levels of phenylalanine and tyrosine. If they're low…I'd say it's PKU. I know you've done a lot of work on paediatric endocrinology. I wondered if you'd oversee the tests and treatment.'

'Sure. If you're right, the parents are going to have to learn to read labels and cut out anything with aspartame in it—phenylalanine's one of its main components, and it's in some medicines as well as sweetened foods and soft drinks. And you'll need to bring in a dietician—they'll have to cut out high-protein foods and restrict starches. A slice of bread can contain over half a day's intake of phenylalanine.' He looked thoughtful. 'She'll need dietary supplements for essential amino acids, vitamins and minerals, and she'll need specially formulated substitute for protein foods. She'll probably also have some attention problems, even with treatment.'

'And if they don't treat it or let her snack on chips and high-protein foods?'

'They'll start seeing behaviour problems, and she'll have problems coping with school.'

'When's it safe to drop the diet?' Zoe asked.

'In theory, once the brain has finished growing and developing. But it's pretty controversial—I'd say right now it's a long-term thing. For the rest of her life. And especially if she decides to have a family when she's older—during pregnancy, if she doesn't keep her levels stable it'll expose the foetus to high levels of phenylalanine, which could cause birth defects, brain damage, or even a miscarriage.'

Good. It had worked. She'd headed him away from personal subjects and onto something safe.

She was just starting to relax again when he said, 'So what *are* you doing tonight?'

Cleaning the house. Tackling the ironing mountain. Anything to stop herself thinking about Brad Hutton. 'I'm meeting Tom.'

'Tom?'

'My boyfriend. The one I was telling you about,' she gabbled.

He raised an eyebrow. 'You don't have a boyfriend.'

How did he know? Unless… No. Judith and Holly wouldn't have told him. Surely they wouldn't. 'Yes, I do,' she lied.

'Zoe—'

'And I'd better get going or I'll be late for our date. It's Friday night, after all. See you later.' And she left before he had a chance to say anything else.

CHAPTER FOUR

ALTHOUGH they were both on duty that weekend, Zoe avoided Brad, except on the ward rounds—and she made sure that he didn't get a chance to speak to her privately about anything.

It drove him bananas. What was it going to take to make her talk to him, tell him the truth? Because he still couldn't work out why she was lying to him, why she was pretending to have a boyfriend. Had she been hurt by someone in the past and no longer trusted men? Or was it something about *him* that worried her? But, if so, what?

Judith and Holly were no help either. He tried asking them. They both shrugged and said, 'Ask Zoe.' Either they really didn't know or they were protecting her. Either way, he was no further forward.

He was still brooding about it on the Monday afternoon—in the guise of doing paperwork in his office—when his phone rang.

'Brad Hutton,' he said, a little more brusquely than he'd intended.

'Hello, Brad. It's Jude. Sorry to bother you—I know you're busy—but I need a paediatrician in Theatre. Like now. Can you send Zoe along, please?'

'No can do.'

There was a second's pause. 'Why not?'

'She's in Theatre already.'

'Oh, no.' The dismay in Judith's voice was palpable. 'Is anyone else available?'

'What's up?'

'I've got a mum with eclampsia.'

The world tilted sharply on its axis. *Eclampsia.* Of all the conditions Brad could have faced in the hospital, it would have to be that one.

'Brad? We're doing an emergency section because the baby's in distress. I need someone over here. Fast,' Judith prompted.

There wasn't anyone else. He couldn't drag Zoe out of Theatre without a lot of explanations he didn't want to give. There was no point in paging his SHO, because she wouldn't be back from her lunch-break on time to make it to Theatre. And he couldn't leave something like this to a house officer who probably hadn't ever seen a case of eclampsia and wouldn't know what to look for in the baby.

So he had to face it himself.

Face the demon that had haunted him for nearly a year.

He felt as if he were talking through a mouthful of sawdust but he managed to force the words out. 'OK. I'm on my way.'

'Thanks. I'm in the delivery suite. Theatre Four,' Judith told him.

Eclampsia. A bolt from the blue because it was impossible to predict who would get it. Although most cases of eclampsia developed from pre-eclampsia, there were also documented cases where the mother hadn't had any signs of pre-eclampsia beforehand. Nobody really knew what caused pre-eclampsia either, though one theory was that it was an abnormality in the body's immune response to pregnancy. It was once called toxaemia of pregnancy but nowadays was known by a longer name reflecting the symptoms, 'hypertension of pregnancy with proteinuria'—in other words, high blood pressure plus protein in the urine.

It had certainly been a bolt from the blue for Lara. She hadn't been in any of the high-risk groups and she'd had good antenatal care. There had been no family history of pre-eclampsia, she hadn't had hypertension, kidney disease or systemic lupus erythematosus before her pregnancy, she had only been having one baby and there had been no problems with the foetus at all during her pregnancy.

Worse still, Lara hadn't actually had pre-eclampsia. No signs of protein in her urine, no swollen fingers or ankles, no signs of high blood pressure. The first either of them had known about it had been when Lara had complained of a headache one afternoon at the office. And then she'd collapsed, had a seizure. By the time she'd been taken to the emergency department and Brad had been paged from Paediatrics, Lara had had two further seizures. Despite the best efforts of the team, the baby hadn't had enough oxygen and she'd died in Lara's womb. His beautiful daughter, the little girl they'd both so looked forward to meeting—dead.

Bile rose in Brad's throat. As if losing his daughter hadn't been enough, that day had turned into his worst nightmare. Because, along with just over a third of women with eclampsia, Lara had developed a complication after delivering their baby. The most common one—a brain haemorrhage—and also the most fatal one.

And so he'd had to arrange a double funeral. His wife and his child. Two coffins—one of them impossibly tiny—that together had contained his whole life. *Ashes to ashes, dust to dust…*

He shook himself. He couldn't go to pieces. Not now. He was a professional, a paediatric consultant, and he had a job to do. He had to look after this baby. Make sure that this one didn't die like Cassandra had.

He scrubbed up and went into Theatre Four.

'Thanks for making it so fast, Brad,' Judith said. 'This is Susie Thornton. She's thirty-seven weeks, it's her first baby and she's thirty-seven.'

Worse and worse. Exactly the same as Lara had been when she'd died. Three years older than he was. First baby, thirty-seven weeks gestation.

'She had moderate pre-eclampsia so we've been keeping a close eye on her on the ward for the last couple of weeks. She's been on bed rest and antihypertensive drugs. She had a bit of a headache, then said it hurt just under her ribs and she thought it might be contractions.'

Brad forced the words through his dry lips. 'And then she had a seizure?'

Judith nodded. 'Textbook case, according to the midwife—thank God she was in the room at the time. Susie stopped breathing, her face twitched, her body became rigid and her muscles started contracting. Then phase two. Convulsions started in her jaw, moved through the muscles of her face and eyelids and spread through her body. The whole thing lasted for just over a minute. She was unconscious for a couple of minutes afterwards, and started hyperventilating when she came round— though she couldn't remember collapsing or having a fit.'

Neither had Lara. When he'd been in the emergency department with her, holding her hand, she'd been distraught. 'What's happening to me, Brad? What happened? I—I can't remember anything. I want our baby to be all right. Promise me our baby will be all right. Don't let anything happen to her.'

Her words echoed through Brad's head, over and over. *Promise me.* And, being a hotshot paediatrician, he'd promised. Of course their baby would be all right. He wouldn't let anything happen to their precious child.

And when it had come to the crunch, he hadn't been able to do a damned thing.

He realised that Judith was still talking him through her patient's history.

'We cleared her airway, made sure she had enough oxygen and put her on her left side so there was a good blood flow to the baby. She's had intravenous magnesium sulphate to prevent any further seizures—it's better than intramuscular, which hurts and leads to abscesses, plus it helps the blood flow to the foetus. I asked for ten-minute obs on her blood pressure and regular checks on proteinuria. I thought she'd stabilised and I was planning to give her oxytocin to induce labour. Susie really wanted a natural birth. But we were monitoring the foetal heart rate, too, and the baby went into distress. Probably because of the antihypertensives. My consultant agreed that we had to deliver. Now.'

'Sure.' Brad's voice was hoarse with effort. 'You'd better keep an eye on her afterwards. In case there's a…' He couldn't say it. Couldn't say the words that had broken his heart. *An intracranial bleed.*

'Complications.' Judith grimaced. 'I'm more worried about the baby. Less than five mums a year die of eclampsia in this country—but it kills ten or eleven babies every week.'

Yeah. He knew that. Knew that the hard way.

This wasn't going to be the same, he told himself fiercely. It wasn't. Yes, it would be another emergency section of a mum with eclampsia. But this time the baby would live. The baby would be fine. The mother would be fine. *Nothing* was going to go wrong.

He watched the anaesthetist checking all the vital signs. Watched Judith make the small incision along the bikini line, watched her partner press down on Susie Thornton's abdomen, watched Judith guide the baby out.

And all the time, he was seeing a different woman. A tall, beautiful blonde who'd held his hand so tightly, so desperately, willing everything to be all right. A woman whose panic had grown in those first seconds after the baby had been delivered—those long, agonising seconds when they'd waited for their little girl to cry. Waited for a sound. Heard the suction as they'd cleared the baby's airways. Waited again for a sound. Still waited as the paediatric team had started CPR. Nothing. Nothing. Nothing.

The baby's cry shocked him into action. Brad forced the bitterness of the past out of his mind and took the baby from Judith's hands.

A little girl. A beautiful little girl. Covered with vernix, the greasy white substance that protected the baby's skin from the amniotic fluid, just as Cassandra had been. But the big difference was that this little girl was crying. Her heart rate was fine. Her muscle tone was fine. She was starting to pink up nicely. She was breathing. He went through his mental checklist and smiled. 'She's got an Apgar of nine,' he said.

A more detailed examination of the baby stopped the panic that had started to beat through him, silenced all the 'what ifs'. 'She's absolutely fine,' he said, handing her to the midwife to be weighed. 'Though I think mum and baby should be in Special Care for the first twenty-four hours. Just to be on the safe side.'

'Standard procedure,' Judith said with a smile. 'Susie's blood pressure should be back to normal within a week, and the protein in her urine should have cleared within six weeks. All being well.'

'Yeah.' Concentrate on the here and now, he told himself, forcing himself to smile back. 'I'd better be getting back to my paperwork,' he said.

'Thanks for your help, Brad.'

'Pleasure.'

Though his smile faded when he left Theatre. Even though this case had turned out all right, hadn't turned into the nightmare he'd lived through last year, it had still unsettled him. Brought back all the memories. Lara's tortured face when she'd learned that their little girl hadn't made it. The bleakness in her eyes. The bitterness in his mouth every time he'd had to explain that, no, he didn't have good news. Their little girl had been stillborn. Phone call after phone call. The more often he'd said it, the more he should have got used to it. But every time the words had cut out another piece of his heart, left him bleeding inside. And when he'd lost Lara as well…

All my pretty chickens and their dam, at one fell swoop?

She'd said it was the most heartbreaking line in *Macbeth*. And he'd learned that the hard way.

He couldn't face the ward. Not right now. Maybe a strong, dark coffee would revive him enough to let him carry on as if nothing was wrong. Maybe.

But when he reached the doors of the staff restaurant, he turned away. He couldn't face that either. Sitting all alone with a cup of coffee while people walked right by him. Here, it would be because they didn't know him. In California, it had been because they hadn't known what to say, and walking straight past him without a word had been easier than trying to stumble through some form of condolences. Some people had even crossed the road rather than talk to him.

A muscle flickered in his jaw. He'd known he'd have to face this at some point in his career. Statistically, he knew he'd face at least one case of eclampsia a year in a major hospital. He'd thought he could handle it, because London City General was a different hospital in a different country, not the one where Lara and Cassandra had died. He'd thought he'd been prepared for it.

How wrong he'd been.

Brad returned to his office on autopilot. Started working through the reports, doggedly concentrating on the words and willing the pain to stay away. He didn't hear the knock on his door. Or the second, louder knock.

Zoe opened the door. 'Are you all right?' she asked.

Of course he wasn't. But he also wasn't up to explaining why.

'What's happened?'

He shook his head.

Zoe closed the door behind her, pulled his blind down and crossed his office in two paces. 'It's better out than in,' she said softly. 'And if you're worried about the office grapevine, I should tell you now that I don't do gossip.'

Yeah. He knew that without having to ask. She might tell Holly and Judith in confidence, if she thought it would help him, but she'd make very sure they kept her confidence.

Even so... 'I'm OK,' he muttered.

'You don't look it.' She took his hand. 'What is it? Bad news from home?'

Home? He didn't have a home any more. He'd sold the house he'd shared with Lara, put most of his things into storage and come over here. To a rented, anonymous flat. A place to live—not home.

'Brad. Talk to me.'

If he didn't, she'd nag him until he did. If he did... No. He didn't want to see the pity in her eyes. Didn't want to see the pity in anyone's eyes. He'd had enough pity to last him several lifetimes.

She rubbed her thumb over the back of his hand, a comforting pressure. 'Is there anyone I can call for you?'

'No.' He didn't have a family any more. Well. In name, perhaps. His older brother, whose reaction to anything bad was to ignore it, pretend it wasn't happening and it would eventually go away. Or his mother, who only ever acknowledged the impact things had on her. He hadn't bothered asking either of them for support after Lara and Cassandra had died, knowing from long experience that he wouldn't get it. His brother would simply have changed the subject, because it was easier to stick his head in the sand than to deal with something painful, and his mother would have sobbed about how much she missed poor dear Lara, how terrible it was not to be a grandmother after all, and whatever was she going to do without them? And Brad would have had to put his own feelings to one side, comfort her when all the time he'd have been crying inside for someone to hold him, comfort him, tell him there was a light at the end of the tunnel and he just had to keep walking towards it.

No.

'There's no one,' he said softly.

'Then talk to *me*,' she said, equally softly.

'There's nothing to tell.'

'I think there is. You look like hell,' she said honestly. 'You're chalk white beneath that tan. What's happened?'

'I had a call to Theatre. A case of eclampsia.'

'That's pretty rare.' She paused. 'I take it you couldn't save the baby?'

No. He hadn't been able to save *his* baby. 'The baby was OK,' he said tonelessly.

'Then what is it?'

The pressure was too much. He snapped. 'Don't you know when to shut up?' he snarled at her.

The silence echoed in his office. She said nothing. Absolutely nothing. But the moment before she turned on her heel to walk out, he saw the look in her eyes. The stricken, wounded look. He'd hurt her. Badly. Without any real justification. She'd tried to make it better and he'd just lashed out.

'I'm sorry, Zoe,' he muttered as she reached the door. 'Don't go. Please.'

He couldn't look at her. He sat at his desk with his head in his hands and just waited for his office door to slam behind her. Instead, he heard a soft click. Well. At least she'd walked out, not stormed out. Maybe tomorrow he could start to repair the damage. Maybe tomorrow he'd buy her flowers, chocolates, apologise properly.

And then a small, gentle hand stroked his forehead.

He nearly leapt a mile out of his chair.

'You're obviously hurting. Badly,' she said, her voice soft and sweet and accepting. 'So I'm going to ignore what you just said to me.'

'I'm sorry. I shouldn't have taken it out on you.'

'You're forgiven.' She sat on the edge of his desk and took his hand. Squeezed it. Held it. 'Provided you give me an explanation.'

He swallowed hard. An explanation. He owed it to her. He knew that. But he had to force the words between lips that felt three times their usual size. 'My wife had eclampsia. She died. So did our baby.'

'When?'

'Last year.' The lump in his throat threatened to suffocate him. 'A year ago next Friday.' And here he was, across the other side of the Atlantic. Not even there to put flowers on their graves. He'd have to get a florist to do that—a florist who had probably never even known Lara, much less knew that freesias had been her favourite flower. Or that he'd bought her freesias every Friday night. Or that the scent of freesias now made him choke.

'That's a tough thing to bear,' she said.

No pity. Just gentle understanding. It was almost too much for him.

But thank God she hadn't said those two terrible words, the words he couldn't handle hearing. *I'm sorry.* How could you possibly be sorry if you hadn't known the person who'd died?

'And that's why you came here? Away from the memories?'

He nodded. 'It was my fault.'

'Eclampsia? No. We don't know who's going to develop it.'

'I should have known. Should have seen the signs.'

'Her midwife should have picked it up before it got that far,' Zoe corrected. 'Blood pressure, protein in the urine—they're the usual signs of pre-eclampsia.'

'Nothing.' He shook his head. 'Lara didn't have pre-eclampsia.'

'Then you, as a doctor, should know how rare that is—and that there's no way you could possibly have predicted it. Besides, you're a paediatrician, not an obstetrician.'

'Exactly. Cassandra… I should have been able to save her. I should have…' That lump again. Choking back his words.

'Cassandra was your little girl?'

He nodded.

Zoe was still holding his hand. 'Were you there when your wife had the seizure?'

'Lara. Her name was Lara.'

'Pretty name. Like the Lara in *Dr Zhivago*.'

'That's what she used to call me. ''Dr Zhivago''. She was a high-school teacher. Taught English lit.' He returned the pressure of Zoe's hand. Right now, he felt as if he were drowning and she was the only one who could stop him going under for the final time.

'Were you with her?' she repeated.

Brad shook his head. 'I was at the hospital. On the ward. They bleeped me. By the time I got there, she'd already had two more seizures. They gave her mag. sulph., thought she'd stabilised. And then they saw the baby was in distress. Gave her a section—she insisted that she wanted a spinal, she didn't want a general, she wanted to be awake when our baby came.' He drew in a shuddering breath. 'But it was too late. Cassandra didn't make it. And Lara blamed herself—maybe if she'd had a general anaesthetic it would have bought Cassandra those few extra moments she'd needed.'

'I doubt it,' Zoe said gently. 'It wasn't Lara's fault. Or yours.'

'I should have kept a closer eye on the monitors.'

'You're not an obstetrician,' she repeated. 'You're a paediatrician.'

'And I didn't save my baby. When she was born, I should have insisted on doing the CPR myself.'

'They wouldn't have let you. Not on your own child,' Zoe reminded him. 'And you already had an important job—being there when Lara needed you. Which you were.'

'I wasn't enough.'

'You're a doctor. Not Superman. Brad, it wasn't your fault. Sometimes these things happen and there isn't a reason or anything or anyone to blame. Sometimes they just happen. You were unlucky.'

'I lost my baby. And then Lara…' The words stuck in

his throat but he had to get them out, had to tell Zoe. 'Lara had a haemorrhage. She didn't make it either. I couldn't save her, Zoe. I couldn't save either of them. What kind of doctor am I?'

'A good one,' she told him. 'One who does his best.'

'My best?' He shook his head. 'But it wasn't good enough.'

'You can't save everyone. You're human. All you can do is your best.' She squeezed his hand. 'And think of all the ones you *do* save. How many lives you've made a difference to. From where I'm sitting, I know which way the scales are tipped.' Her mouth compressed for a moment, and then she nodded, as if she'd come to some kind of decision. 'You need to get out of here.'

'I've got paperwork to do.'

'Paperwork can wait. Come on. Let's go.' She slid off his desk.

'What about your shift?'

'It ended half an hour ago. As did yours.'

'Where are we going?'

'To get some food. And some quiet—where you can talk in peace.'

Giovanni's? Hardly. Though he couldn't think where else she meant. Couldn't think straight, full stop.

But he knew he could trust Zoe.

So let Hurricane Zoe steer him wherever she would.

CHAPTER FIVE

BRAD recognised the gate as soon as Zoe stopped—the wrought-iron gate she'd closed so very firmly between them when he'd walked her home from Giovanni's. She'd brought him here? To her home? But she'd said something about food. She was cooking for him?

He still couldn't take anything in—couldn't think for the pain that surged through every single nerve end, that throbbed through his blood with every beat of his heart. He was only dimly aware that there was a black and red chequered path to her front door, and the hallway echoed the same theme with black and white chequered tiles. High ceilings, old gold walls, a bentwood coatstand, framed prints of Pre-Raphaelite art—and then she'd hung his coat on the stand and was ushering him through to the kitchen.

'Sit,' she said, pointing at one of the chairs next to the glass-topped table. The next thing he knew, a glass of red wine was in front of him.

'I don't—it's early—I...' Hell. He couldn't even string three words together.

'Not *that* early, and I'm not planning to let you get completely plastered. You're going to be eating with that, whether you like it or not. Take a big sip, then a deep breath. Then talk. It doesn't matter what you say—I won't be passing it on to anyone. But you need to talk, Brad. Don't keep it locked inside any more.'

She was bossy. *Incredibly* bossy. But, right now, that was exactly what he needed. And she had a point. He did need to talk. He'd kept it inside for so long now, it was starting to destroy him.

He took a sip of the wine and glanced around her kitchen. It had an almost Mediterranean feel about it— white walls, large terracotta tiles on the floor, pale olive-green units and darker green worktops. Restful. A place to call home.

Zoe wasn't looking at him. She was pottering around the kitchen, taking things out of cupboards and the fridge, finding a knife and a chopping board, picking sprigs of herbs from the pots growing along the window-sill. Acting as if everything was perfectly normal.

He knew exactly what she was doing. Giving him the space he needed, not staring earnestly at him with pity on her face. And he could have kissed her for it.

No. *Not* kiss. Zoe was offering him friendship, not a quick lay! And, yes, he did find Zoe attractive. But he'd just fallen apart in the middle of the ward, over a case almost exactly like the one that had ripped his happiness from him a year ago. He was in no fit state to kiss anyone.

Hell. His emotions were so tangled right now, he didn't know what he wanted. Just that he wanted…something. He wanted to be held. He wanted someone to tell him that everything was going to be all right. He wanted Zoe.

'Tell me about Lara,' Zoe said softly. 'What was she like?'

He took another deep breath. Talk about Lara. He'd hardly been able to talk about her since she'd died. This was going to hurt, he knew. And yet, as soon as he opened his mouth, he found it didn't. It was OK, talking to Zoe about her. Safe. 'She was clever and funny and beautiful,' he said. 'She had these amazing blue eyes. They were the first thing I noticed about her. I met her on the ward.' Easier and easier. He was even smiling, instead of inwardly raging about her loss. Instead of pummelling a cushion until his hands hurt and asking, 'Why? Why her?'

'She was supporting her sister. Her three-year-old niece was in with meningitis and Lara came in every day to make Nell rest for a couple of hours instead of sitting at Sadie's bedside.'

'Just the kind of family we like most in Paeds,' Zoe agreed. 'So you were looking after Sadie?'

'Yes. It turned out to be Hib.'

Zoe winced. 'Nasty. And rare.' Hib was short for *Haemophilus influenzae*, type b, a serious disease that mainly affected babies and children up to the age of four.

'Nell had got worried about vaccinations, with all the scares about whether shots caused more harm than they cured. She didn't have Sadie's vaccinations done, and she was unlucky.'

'But Sadie recovered?'

Brad nodded. 'She was lucky—she didn't end up with post-meningitis deafness. But she was in my ward for a while, and I got talking to Lara. I found myself looking for her. And then I noticed she didn't wear a ring. So when Sadie was discharged, I asked Lara out on a date. She said yes, and it just worked between us. She didn't mind that I wasn't a nine-to-fiver, that my hours could be a bit strange—when I was working lates, she could mark assignments.'

'What did she teach again?'

'English lit at high school. She introduced me to the theatre.'

'Sounds good.' Zoe slid a tray into the oven. 'Ciabatta bread OK with you? Sorry it's not my own.'

'It's fine. Thanks.'

'When did you first realise you were in love with her?'

'At the theatre. She'd taken me to see *Much Ado About*

Nothing. And every word that Benedick said about Beatrice…that was how I felt about Lara. I walked her home in the snow. And then it stopped snowing just long enough for a star to come out.' He closed his eyes at the memory. 'The wishing star. I asked her to marry me, under the wishing star. We got married three months later.'

He heard the sound of Zoe's chair scraping the floor as she came to sit opposite him. 'Were you married long?'

'Nearly five years.' That's all they'd had. Five short years. He opened his eyes again. 'She was three years older than me but we thought we had plenty of time to start a family. We just enjoyed being together. We'd been married eighteen months when she told me we were expecting a baby. We hadn't planned it, but I was thrilled. I really wanted to be a dad. She had a miscarriage at ten weeks, so we agreed to wait a while before trying again. But it took ages the next time. We were at the point where we were going for tests to find out if either of us had a problem when she said she felt strange. She did a test and it was positive.' His throat closed as he remembered the sheer joy in Lara's eyes as she'd told him. His own answering whoop, how he'd picked her up and whirled her round, then suddenly panicked. How he'd wrapped Lara in cotton wool throughout her pregnancy.

He dragged in a shuddering breath. 'You know the rest.'

'Yes.' Again, Zoe didn't say she was sorry. But she took his hand and squeezed it. Comforting him. 'It's tough when you lose someone you love.'

There was an odd note in her voice and he looked at her. Had she lost someone she loved, too? Was that why he could see understanding in her eyes instead of pity? He'd have sworn she was in professional doctor mode if it hadn't been for her voice. Zoe Kennedy knew what pain was. And gut instinct told him she knew how to hide it, too.

'It was afterwards that was bad. I just felt numb. Lost. There was this gaping hole in my life and I didn't know how to fill it, except with work. But there were too many memories. Memories of her meeting me from my shift during the school vacations, or we'd go out to lunch, or she'd surprise me with tickets to a movie. I even took her ice-skating once, and it was like she'd been born to it. She had this natural grace, this poise.'

A grace and poise that Zoe knew she didn't have. She stamped on the little flutterings of jealousy. Right now, this wasn't about her. This was about giving Brad some space. Letting him talk. Helping him heal all the hurt inside. 'She was a good skater?'

'She looked like a princess. She was only wearing jeans and a sloppy Joe, but she could have been in lace and silk and spangles and a tiara. It was just the way she moved. I'd been planning to show off—I'd skated for years—but she took my breath away. And I fell over. Flat on my face.'

Zoe could just imagine it, and smiled. 'I hope she laughed.'

'She did.' Brad looked at her. 'I haven't ever told anyone about that.'

'Maybe it's time you did.' Hadn't his family rallied round him, held him close and helped him cope in those first dark days after his loss? Something in his face stopped her asking. Another layer of pain that he couldn't bear to expose yet, she guessed. And she wanted to help him, not hurt him more.

'She'd have been a good mum. The best. There whenever Cassie fell over and skinned her knees, ready to kiss it better. Sitting in the front row at the school play, mopping her eyes and clapping the loudest at the end. Reading endless stories and giving cuddles when Cassie couldn't sleep. She'd have done all that and more.'

'It's all the things you never had a chance to do that hurt the most,' she said. She'd learned that, too. Regrets for what had happened were nothing compared to the longing for what might have been. The things you hadn't had time to share.

'I miss her, Zoe. I miss her. And I miss my little girl. I only held her once. She was so beautiful. She'd have had her mother's smile. And I never got the chance to see it. Never got the chance to see my little girl grow up, to hear her call me "Daddy".'

There was nothing Zoe could say. Because what he'd just said applied to her, too. Ten years ago, she'd made her decision. And even though sometimes her biological clock started ticking and she found herself getting just that little bit clucky over the smallest patients on the ward, she had to suppress it. Hard. And steel herself against the knowledge that she would never have a child of her own, never hear herself called 'Mummy', never come home to her partner's arms and a kiss hello that said a lot more than that.

But this way she didn't get the pain either. She wouldn't see the pity in her would-be lover's eyes, see it shift to embarrassment and then revulsion.

Damaged goods.

The words echoed in her head.

'Hang in there,' she said softly, almost as much to herself as to Brad. And she moved over to the oven before he could see the tears glittering in her eyes. She blinked hard as she put the ciabatta bread in to crisp, put plates to warm in the top oven and tipped the tray of roasted vegetables into the tomato sauce. If he noticed anything, she'd claim it was the heat from the oven.

'I've been hanging in there for so long,' he told her, his voice almost a rasp, 'I sometimes think I've forgotten what the world even feels like.'

She turned the temperature down on the hob and returned to the table. 'It's still there. Right around you. And every day you do your job, you give someone else the hope you've forgotten about. Maybe you just need to look at what you do, really see what it is you're giving. And remember that what goes around comes around.'

'Please, don't tell me you're going to say time's a healer.'

'It isn't. You just learn how to deal with the pain.'

'I wasn't very gracious to people,' he said. 'When they told me Lara wouldn't have wanted me to lock myself away, that I was still young and Lara would have wanted me to meet someone else, that Lara wouldn't have wanted me to grieve like that...' He shook his head in apparent frustration. 'How the hell would *they* know what she thought?'

'They didn't. They couldn't. They were just trying to help, and it was something to say. Something to fill the silence.'

'I couldn't handle their pity.'

'That's not what I'm offering.' She patted his hand. 'Right, you can make yourself useful and lay the table. The cutlery's in the drawer over there.' While he set the table, she drained the pasta, divided it between the warmed plates and topped it with the sauce. 'Grate your own cheese,' she said, putting the pasta in front of him and then bringing over a hunk of Parmesan and a grater.

He waited for her to bring the bread over and sit down

opposite him, then took a forkful of pasta. 'This is seriously good. Thank you.'

'*Prego*, as my Italian grandmother would say.'

'I didn't know your grandmother was Italian.'

Zoe wrinkled her nose. 'She isn't. But if she was Italian, that's what she'd say.'

'You're crazy.' There was a glimmer of a smile on his face. Just a glimmer. But her heart gave an answering surge. Brad was in what seemed like a pit of despair—and she'd been the one to make him smile again.

'Crazy?' She spread her hands. 'Hurricane Zoe. Thar she blows.'

He eyed her speculatively. 'Did you really go paddling in the middle of winter?'

'Yes.'

'You actually *wanted* to paddle in ice-cold water?'

'No.'

'Then...what?'

'Let's just say a friend of mine was feeling bad. I wanted to make her smile again. So I dragged her out for a bracing walk on the beach—you need sunglasses in winter, too, by the way, to stop the sand blowing in your eyes and stinging like mad—and made her talk to me.'

'Where does the paddling come into it?'

'Desperation, on my part. But it worked. She talked. She smiled. And she's moved on from the bad times.'

'So you do this for all your friends? Let them cry on your shoulder?'

'If they need to, yes. I give them room to talk, and they know it's not going any further. And then I feed them.'

He tore a chunk from the hot loaf, and Zoe had to stop watching his hands. Because it was only too easy to imagine Brad's head on her shoulder. And his hands stroking her skin, touching her, making her feel—

No. No touching. Definitely no touching. She couldn't risk that.

'What about you?' he asked.

'What about me?'

'Whose shoulder do you cry on when you need to?'

My own. Not that she was going to tell him that. Nobody at London City General knew when she cried or why, and she was going to keep it that way. 'I have some good friends.' Let him infer what he wanted from that.

'Thank you,' he said when he'd cleared his plate. 'I didn't realise how much I needed that.'

I need something, too, Zoe's heart whispered, but she wrapped her arms around herself to muffle it. 'My pleasure,' she said. 'And I was cooking for myself anyway, so you weren't causing me any trouble, before you say it.'

'Can I wash up for you? As my very pitiful contribution?'

'Yes, please. And then we'll have pudding.' Good. She'd got herself back under control again. Bouncy, happy, Zoe. Chubby, cheerful and completely WYSIWYG. What you saw was exactly what you got. As long as you didn't peek beneath the smiley layer.

Washing up with Brad felt strangely intimate. Even stranger, it felt right for him to be there with her. As if he belonged there.

Just friends, remember? she warned herself.

She wiped up the last bit of crockery and put it away, then put the tea-towel straight into the washing machine. 'Right, Mr Hutton. I think you've earned pudding.' She dug in the top drawer of her freezer. 'Um. You have a choice of maple pecan or maple pecan.'

He smiled. A real smile. Only a little one, but it was there. 'Maple pecan will do just fine.' He glanced at the packaging. 'Real American ice-cream.'

'The best. Except for…' She paused.

'Your Italian grandmother's?'

She grinned. 'Something like that. Actually, I was going to say my own. But the strawberries have to be from Norfolk, from the farm round the corner from my aunt's cottage, so I only make it in summer.' She looked at him. 'Are we going to do this the proper way, or the prim-and-proper way?'

'There's only one way to eat ice-cream. Straight from the tub.'

'A man after my own heart. Good.' She took two spoons from the drawer. 'Sofa, I think.'

Brad followed her into the living room. Like the rest of the house he'd seen so far, it was simply furnished and the colours were plain, this time a deep green carpet, pale terracotta walls and curtains with tiny green leaves on them. Her cushions matched the carpet, and were flung casually onto a dark terracotta sofa.

'It's a William Morris print,' she said, noticing his gaze. 'Appropriate, really, since he was born just down the road and the house is Victorian.'

'It's lovely.' It was. High ceilings teamed with ornate cornicing and a sense of space. He liked it. It felt like home.

She followed his gaze to the ceiling rose. 'OK. So I'm boring and my ceiling's white. But you'd understand if you saw the place Jude, Holls and I rented as students.'

'What was so bad about it?' He stretched out on the sofa while she switched her CD player on.

'It had this incredible ceiling rose—and someone had painted every single flower a different colour, and the leaves two-tone green. Every time I looked up, I vowed I was going to paint it white, but in the end it became a kind of talking point among our friends.'

'Right.' He took the lid off the ice-cream and offered her first scoop. 'I like this music. What is it?'

'Corelli. It's the Concerto Grosso in D. Jude got me into this—she did it for an exam, and she used to play it when she was revising. I think because it's so regular, it's perfect to chill out to.'

'Definitely.' He took another spoonful of ice-cream. Crazy. He was sitting on a sofa with a woman he hardly knew. He'd told her things he'd never told anyone else. And for the first time since Lara had died, his heart actually felt lighter. The tunnel was still long, still dark, but there was a definite chink of light at the end of it. All thanks to Zoe. He was coming back to life.

'So do you eat ice-cream like this often?'

'With Jude and Holls. I can't *quite* manage a whole tub on my own.'

But surely men were lining up to eat ice-cream with Zoe Kennedy? She had everything. She was clever, she was charming, she was cheerful. She cooked like an angel.

And he wanted to find out more. What made her tick. What she dreamed about. And why she pretended to have a boyfriend—not that she appeared to be pretending right now. She hadn't mentioned 'Tom' since she'd brought him here. Brad took another spoonful of ice-cream and his spoon clashed with hers.

'Mine,' he said.

She screwed her nose up. 'That's greedy.'

'Open your mouth.' The words came out before he even realised he'd been thinking them.

She opened her mouth.

And Brad slid his spoon inside. Let her lick the ice-cream from the spoon.

'My turn,' he said, opening his mouth.

She rose to the challenge, dipping her spoon into the carton and then feeding the creamy confection to him.

'Yours.' He took a spoonful of ice-cream and rubbed the back of the spoon along her lower lip.

'Yours.' She did the same. Her voice, he noticed, was a few tones lower. There were definite amber glints in her eyes. And he was filled with an insane urge to find out what she tasted like. He needed to kiss her. Now.

He leaned forward and touched his mouth to hers. Gently. So gently that their lips barely met. Again. And again, this time a little bolder. She made a small sound in the back of her throat and the next thing he knew he was nibbling her lower lip until she sighed her acquiescence and opened her mouth, letting him kiss her properly.

Kissing wasn't enough. He needed to touch her, hold her. And the way she was responding to him, her fingers threading through his hair, she needed this, too.

He smoothed his hands down her back and then slid one hand underneath the hem of her jersey top. His fingertips connected with bare skin, soft and warm and smooth and tempting him on. Slowly, gently, he let his hand drift upwards.

And Zoe pulled away. 'No. We can't do this.'

Was it his imagination, or was there a note of panic in her voice? 'Zoe?'

She smoothed her top down again. 'We're colleagues. We have to work together. We…we can't do this sort of thing.'

'I— You're right. I'm sorry. I was acting unprofessionally.'

'No. It's my fault. I made you talk to me about Lara. It's stirred up your emotions and here we are sitting together on the sofa, eating ice-cream. Of course you'd…well…um.'

She was gabbling and they both knew it.

Something had frightened her, upset her. Brad didn't know what it was or how to fix it or even how to find out what she was hiding, but he knew one thing: she was in his life now, and he didn't want her to go away again. 'I'm sorry. I had no intention of upsetting you or insulting you, Zoe.'

'You haven't.'

'So we're still colleagues?' He took a risk. 'Still friends?'

There was still a hint of panic in her eyes, but she nodded.

'Good. I, um, I'd better go.' Hell. He'd never felt this awkward before. 'I'll see you tomorrow at work?'

'Yes.'

'And, Zoe?' He paused. 'Thank you for tonight.' For pushing the demons away—not that he wanted to say it. He hoped she could see it in his face.

'No problem.'

'I'll see myself out.'

'Sure.'

Zoe stayed on the sofa until she heard the door close quietly behind Brad. Then she brought her knees up and wrapped her arms round her legs, resting her chin on her knees. She should never have accepted that spoonful of ice-cream. Should never have kissed him back. Her mouth was still tingling from where he'd kissed her and she could still taste him.

She squeezed her eyes tightly shut, willing the tears to stay back. She couldn't have what she wanted. Never would have it. And although she was almost burning up with longing, it would pass. It had to. Because the alternative was much, much worse. He'd said it himself: *I couldn't handle their pity.* And once he knew the truth about her…pity would be all he'd be able to offer. All any man would offer her. And she really, really didn't want that.

CHAPTER SIX

ZOE managed to keep things on a professional footing with Brad for the next day, and then she had two days off—enough, she hoped, to put a bit of distance between them. At least he didn't try to contact her while she was off—she needed time to get herself back to normal.

The problem was, she couldn't forget that kiss. Couldn't forget the way he'd teased her with the ice-cream and then kissed her. Properly.

One kiss was all it had taken to bring her hormones zooming back to life. And she just couldn't let it happen. Be sensible, she told herself. Yes, you like him. A lot. But you can't offer him anything more than friendship. Keep it cool for now. Once you're back at work, things can go back to normal.

Couldn't they?

Brad, in turn, discovered that he missed Zoe— he seemed to have developed this built-in radar that told him when she was around. He missed her when she wasn't on the ward. And then it was Friday. The day he'd been dreading. He'd thought about working through it, on the grounds that being busy on the ward would mean he had no time to brood. But he knew he'd find it too hard to be kind, smiley, *nice* Brad Hutton on the day his scars opened up again. On the day when he asked a florist to put freesias on Lara's grave, thousands of miles away. So he took the day off.

In the end he spent it mooching round the British

Museum on his own, lingering in the manuscript room as Lara would no doubt have done, then walking through the Elgin marbles, marvelling at the way the sculptor had caught the flare of a horse's nose, the wind rustling through a mane.

When at last his feet ached, he walked through the shop towards the café—and saw the little book of Christina Rossetti's poems. Lara's favourite. On impulse, he bought it. And when he sat down with a latte, he flicked through the little book. His breath caught as he read the words:

> *And afterwards remember. Do not grieve…*
> *Better by far, you should forget and smile*
> *Than that you should remember and be sad.*

It could have been Lara talking directly to him. Telling him that it was time to move on. *Remember, do not grieve.*

Maybe, just maybe, this was a sign. Lara had been his other half. But he was still only thirty-five. He had half a lifetime ahead of him, and it was time for him to live again. To love again. To find happiness, like the joy he'd found with Lara.

And there was one person he could imagine doing that with. Zoe Kennedy. She was very different from Lara, more outgoing and full of madcap ideas. But there was something special about her and he'd liked her from the moment he'd met her. Felt drawn to her even. He thought she felt that same pull, but there was something stopping her from acting on it. Something that had made her pull away in a panic when he'd kissed her. So she had demons to face, too.

Maybe they could face them together. Maybe not. Brad closed the poetry book and finished his coffee. Tonight he'd remember Lara. Remember the good times and be glad. And tomorrow... Tomorrow, maybe he'd talk to Zoe. Take the first tentative steps towards what he hoped would be their future.

When he got home, there was a message on his answering-machine. 'Hi, this is Zoe. I know what today is, so I just thought I'd ring and say I was thinking of you. If you want to talk or anything, I'm around.'

No. He didn't want to talk today. But maybe tomorrow...

'Morning, Brad. You OK?' Zoe asked in her best casual tone. She deliberately didn't ask if he'd had a good day off. She knew it wouldn't have been a good day for him, whatever he'd done.

'Yeah. I'm fine.' To her surprise, he sounded as if he meant it—not as if he was trying to make it true by saying it. And then he smiled at her. The kind of smile that made her knees refuse to work. 'Thanks for your message. I appreciated it.'

'Any time.' If she wasn't careful, this could start straying over the boundaries she'd set herself. She switched to a safer topic: work. 'I've checked Andy Solomon's X-rays and he's doing well. He's not going to need surgery and I think we can release him to his GP's care.' She smiled. 'He's pretty desperate to go home now—the novelty's definitely worn off.'

'OK, I'll sign his discharge forms and do the letter for the GP. Anyone else?'

'Sanjay and Sanjeev.' The four-month-old twins had been admitted with Respiratory Syncytial Virus, or RSV, a week before. 'They're off oxygen and their feeding's nearly back to normal levels. Temp, respiration and pulse are all fine. And it'll really make Rupinder's weekend if she can take them home today.' She handed him the files. 'And that's it for now. I've got a drug round to sort out.'

'Have fun. Come and grab me when you're ready for a coffee—I owe you one.'

'Sure.'

Though then there was an influx of admittances, so she didn't have time. And that set the tone for the next week—quick case conferences, one or the other of them promising coffee or lunch but never getting the time.

The following Friday morning, they were both rostered on PAU. Zoe's first case was a small girl with severe eczema—the itch had been so bad that the little girl had scratched herself until she'd bled.

'I feel guilty about bringing Flora here,' Joanne Kelly said, 'but I've been to my GP so many times about it, and all he says is that I should give her warm baths and use lots of emollient. But it's not working, and I...' She was clearly only just holding back the tears, Zoe thought, and her suspicions were confirmed when Joanne added in a whisper, 'I just don't know what else to do. The doctor makes me feel as if I'm making a fuss over nothing, but the itching's so *bad*. She wakes up in the night, crying. I give her baby paracetamol, but it doesn't help much. I can't remember the last time I had a proper night's sleep—even if she's not itching, I'm half-awake, just waiting for her to wake up and scratch and start crying. Just look at her arms. She's covered in scratches. I keep her nails short, I tell her not to scratch, but she's not two yet—how can I expect her to understand?'

'And of course she'll scratch, because the itch is annoying her. When she's older, she'll learn to pinch or press her skin, not scratch,' Zoe said.

'I can't even take her to toddler group.' Joanne bit her lip. 'The other kids stare at her and I can see the other mums whispering together and wondering if their kids are going to get a rash like hers if they play with her.'

'Eczema's not contagious,' Zoe reassured her. 'But that doesn't help you right now. Did your GP refer you to a dermatologist or a dietician?'

'No. But I know Flora reacts to milk and eggs. I've tried giving her goat's milk but that doesn't make any difference.'

'It often doesn't, though it's always worth a try. I'm going refer you for dermatology tests so we can see exactly what Flora's reacting to, and to a dietician as well so if she's allergic to any other foods you can avoid them and still make sure she's getting the nutrients she needs to grow properly.'

'So it isn't me?'

'No. But your GP did tell you to do the right thing. Emollient cream will stop Flora's skin losing water and prevent it being so dry—it acts as a kind of barrier and will stop her skin feeling so dry and itchy. But you'll probably need to try out several to see which works best for her.' Zoe smiled at Joanne. 'I assume you're already using cotton bedding for her, not synthetic or wool?'

'And I'm using non-biological powder in the wash and steering clear of fabric conditioner,' Joanne confirmed.

'Great. We need to stop the scratching, too—it's an itch-scratch-itch cycle. The more she itches, the more she scratches—and that inflames her skin and makes it feel as if it's itching more. So she scratches more and ends up like this. As well as being frightening for her and upsetting for you, if the skin breaks there's a chance that bacteria will get in and cause a secondary infection. She probably won't keep mittens on at night, so you could try wet-wrapping—it'll stop the itching, act as a barrier so she can't get to her skin, and it'll also help any treatment creams sink deeper into the skin so they work better. I can get one of the nurses to teach you how to do that. Did your GP prescribe any steroid cream?'

'No. Whenever he's seen us, her skin's been getting better. I think he reckons I'm one of those mums who use their children's illness to get attention. He's one of the old school—actually, he's a bit scary.'

'It's important that you feel you can talk to your GP. If you can't talk to him, you can always ask to see another doctor at the practice,' Zoe suggested gently. 'I'm going to prescribe some steroid cream for Flora—this isn't steroids as in bodybuilders but corticosteroids, which the body produces naturally. It can thin the skin if you use strong creams over a long period of time, but if you use it when Flora's having a bad flare-up like this, and use it very thinly, you should be fine.'

'And she's not going to end up with scars all over her face?'

'Not if you use the steroid cream properly,' Zoe reassured her. 'You need to put it on the worst areas, not all of her skin, and the best time to put it on her is straight after she's had a bath, when her skin's hydrated.'

Joanne relaxed visibly. 'I just didn't want her to grow up and be treated like a freak. Kids can be so cruel, and if she was covered in scars, they'd…'

Oh, yes. Zoe knew all about that. And it wasn't just kids who could be cruel. Even if it wasn't deliberate, seeing pity and revulsion in people's eyes could hurt just as much. That, and then seeing the sneaking, guilty relief that it had happened to someone else and not them…

She stamped on her feelings. Hard. She was Dr Zoe Kennedy, paediatric registrar. And she was meant to be helping Flora, not wallowing in her own past miseries. 'She'll be fine,' she said lightly. 'The good news is, she's likely to grow out of it—four out of five children who have severe eczema find it's improved a lot by the time they're fourteen. When she's an adult, she might only have occasional flare-ups or reactions.'

'So this isn't going to be for ever?'

'No,' Zoe reassured her. 'Now I've referred you, you'll see the dermatologist regularly and there may be other treatments you can try if the steroids aren't effective enough—there's a new ointment out now called tacrolimus, though I think it's only licensed for children over two. The dermatologist will know a lot more about it than I do.'

'Thank you.'

'No problem. I'll introduce you to Erin, our paediatric nurse, and she'll show you how to apply the cream and do wet-wrapping.' Zoe ruffled Flora's hair. 'We'll have you feeling better soon, little one.'

She left them in Erin's care with the prescription for corticosteroid cream, and went to see her next patient. Between the assessment room and the cubicles, she saw Brad a couple of times but not for long enough to do more than smile or exchange a brief, polite pleasantry.

Things were completely back to normal between them, the kiss forgotten—clearly so on his part, though she couldn't quite push it out of her mind. As for that odd sinking feeling in her stomach—something akin to disappointment—well, that would pass. She'd make it pass. Because a relationship between them was completely out of the question.

At least she had something to look forward to tonight: the drive to Norfolk for a girly weekend with Holly and Judith. A walk on the beach was exactly what she needed right now. The wind would blow out the cobwebs. And, with them, any stupid ideas she might still be harbouring about Brad Hutton.

At half past two, she was called to the phone. 'Zo? It's Jude. The ward said you were on PAU today.'

'All set for tonight?' Zoe asked brightly.

'Um, that's why I'm calling.' Judith sighed. 'All hell's been let loose down here. I think there must have been an amazing party nine months ago because we've got babies galore! Sally called in sick today with flu—I'd per-suaded Rowan to cover for me for the weekend, but he looks like death warmed up and I think he's coming down with it, too, and—'

'No way can you risk that level of infection around newborns. So you've got to work this weekend,' Zoe fin-ished.

'I'm sorry, Zo. I was really looking forward to it. I know it's late to call off. But if I go, we're going to be really short-staffed this weekend. I can't be that selfish.'

'Of course you can't.' Zoe tried to wipe the disappoint-ment from her voice.

'You and Holls can still have a good time without me. I'd got us a box of gianduja—you can pick it up on your way out tonight. Just be noble and save me one out of the box, OK?'

Ordinarily, Zoe would have jumped at the offer; she adored gianduja, the mix of toasted hazelnuts and cocoa butter that Judith had discovered in Turin one year and brought back for her best friends. But today wasn't 'or-dinarily'. 'Actually, Holls rang me earlier. She's had to cancel, too.'

'Oh, no. Why?'

'Family problems.'

'Right.' It was their shared shorthand for Holly's brother. Five years younger than Holly, Daniel had fallen in with a bad crowd at school and had ended up taking drugs. He'd eventually dropped out of college and worried his parents sick, and Holly had been the only one able to reach him and nag him into rehabilitation. Since then, Daniel had been clean most of the time, but every so often he had a relapse. And that meant Holly had to bail him out. 'So she's going back to Liverpool?'

'She caught the train at lunch-time.'

'Oh, Zo. Look, I'll see if I can get someone to—'

'No, it's OK. I might go on my own.'

'The gianduja's here, if you want it,' Judith offered.

'Thanks, but I think we'll need it more when Holls gets back.'

'Yeah. You're right. And lots and lots of coffee.' Judith sighed. 'I'll talk to you later, Zo. And I'm sorry.'

'You're my best friend,' Zoe reminded her. 'You don't have to apologise.'

She'd just replaced the receiver when Brad came over. 'Everything OK, Zoe?'

Her disappointment obviously showed on her face. She never would make a good poker player. She shrugged. 'Just a change of plan. I was supposed to be going away with Holls and Jude this weekend, but something's come up and they can't make it. So the trip's cancelled.' She should have left it there, but somehow her mouth opened and the words came out. 'Unless you fancy a weekend at the seaside?'

'This is the place where you paddle in the middle of winter, right?'

'Yes.'

He grinned. 'Then, thanks. I'd love to.'

Damn. He should have said no. But she did have one get-out. 'Um, I should have checked. Are you on duty?'

'On call,' he corrected, 'but that's not a problem.'

He was just going to leave Paeds in the lurch?

'I'll find someone to swap with me,' he said softly.

Zoe felt heat shoot into her cheeks. Of course he would. Brad was too responsible to do anything else. She just wasn't thinking straight. Not thinking at all, or she wouldn't have asked him to go away with her. 'Right. Um, it'll give you a chance to see a bit of the country while you're here,' she said. She had to make it very clear that she'd asked him as a friend and she wasn't making a pass at him.

'Thanks for asking me.'

'Pleasure.' The perfect cue, she thought with relief. 'That's what friends are for, isn't it?' So now he knew the terms: friends only. 'I'll meet you outside the front entrance to the hospital at half past four.'

'Great. What do I need to bring?'

'Just yourself and a change of clothes.'

The rest of her shift passed in a blur. And then it was half past four. She drove up to the hospital entrance and Brad was waiting for her, leaning casually against the wall, a holdall and a carrier bag next to him. She caught her breath. In jeans, a cream sweater, desert boots and a black leather jacket, he looked absolutely edible. She was going to have to be very careful this weekend.

Remember, she told herself, this is strictly friends.

He put his luggage in the boot of her car, then climbed into the passenger seat. 'I take it you don't need a map-reader?' he asked.

'No. But I'll let you fiddle with the CD player.'

He flicked through her collection of CDs as she drove them out of East London. 'Hmm. Promising. But I'm sure Holly told me you had a tin ear.'

'I do. They won't let me sing.'

'I could teach you.'

She was very glad she had to concentrate on the road. Because if she had to look at him after an offer like that, she would definitely make a fool of herself. *I could teach you.* Said in that sultry voice, it could mean a lot of things...

No. He was only there as a substitute for Holly and Judith. So she was going to treat him as an honorary female.

Get real, a little voice scorned in her head. Brad Hutton is all male, and you know it. 'I'm beyond teaching. Jude's already tried,' she said lightly.

'Tell me more about where we're going,' Brad said.

'The village is called Marsh End—it's on the edge of the salt marshes,' she told him. 'The beach there is a wildlife sanctuary—it's a bird-watcher's haven. Holls, Jude and I normally go to the nearest town, Brandham-on-sea, for a walk along the pier then along the beach itself and climb over the breakwaters. A woolly mammoth was discovered a few years ago in the cliffs near Brandham, though the three of us have never managed to find any fossils. Last time we went, Jude took pity on me and bought me an ammonite from the geology shop.'

'So you're a secret fossil-hunter?'

'I used to do it a lot when I was a teenager.' In the year she'd had to take out of school. The year when she'd lived with her aunt by the sea until her ribs had finally knitted together and her scars had healed. On the surface, at least. 'I did some metal-detecting, too. I wanted to uncover a Roman settlement.'

'By the sea?'

'Don't scoff. Norfolk's the land of Boudicca, queen of the Iceni—the warrior queen who rebelled against the Romans. Caister, just down the road from Brandham, was a Roman camp. And at Holme, a bit further north along the coast, they found Seahenge. It's a wooden circle, more or less the equivalent of Stonehenge, and it's four thousand years old, dating from the start of the Bronze Age.'

'I take it you never found your Roman camp, though?'

'Not even a coin. Just empty soft drink cans and bits of tin foil,' she admitted ruefully.

He chuckled. 'So are we going treasure-hunting tomorrow?'

'Nope. Just walking by the sea and poking around in rock pools. Then having fish and chips—we can eat them on the end of the pier, if it's not raining.'

'Sounds good to me.'

Zoe found herself relaxing with Brad, telling him more about the part of the country she loved best. And when he started singing to one of the CDs, she relaxed completely, enjoying the sound of his voice as she drove.

Brad gave Zoe a sidelong look. To his relief, she was smiling. Back to the Zoe he'd first met, instead of the wary stranger he'd worked with since he'd kissed her. He'd liked the way she'd shared her teenage dreams with him. She clearly adored the north Norfolk coast—maybe she'd let her guard down still further with him when she was on home territory. And he really wanted to get to know Zoe properly. Understand what made her tick. And maybe even why she was so scared of being kissed. Maybe. But for now he was happy just to be with her.

They stopped at a pub just outside Cambridge for dinner, then drove through the thick pine forest that heralded the start of Norfolk. Nearly three quarters of an hour after they'd skirted around Norwich, Zoe pulled into the driveway of a flint-and-brick cottage.

'This is it,' she said. 'My Aunt Jay lived here ever since I can remember—but she fell in love with a wine importer about five years ago and he whisked her over to France. She's kept the cottage as her base in England, and lets the family use it as a holiday cottage. We take turns in the summer, but in the winter it's more or less all mine. Jay gets one of the neighbours to keep an eye on the place and give it an airing if nobody's been here for a couple of weeks. I let Mrs Harris know when I'm coming here, and she turns the heating up for me.'

'It's charming,' Brad said as he helped Zoe unload the car.

'Mind your head. It's three hundred years old, so the doorways are on the low side,' Zoe warned. She grinned. 'That's when it's useful, not being tall.' She unlocked the door, switched on the light and ushered him in.

It was everything Brad expected an English country cottage to be—pale walls, floral-print curtains, stripped woodwork and filled with the scent of beeswax and roses and lavender from the polished wood and the bowls of pot-pourri dotted around the cottage.

'I brought these as my contribution,' he said, handing the carrier bag to her.

Zoe unpacked the bottles of wine. 'Thanks.' Her smile broadened when she saw the box of Italian chocolates. 'Yum. Thank you even more. I love these—almost as much as gianduja.'

'Gianduja?'

'That's what Jude normally brings for our weekends here,' she explained.

So now he knew one way to her heart. Not that he was stupid enough to say it.

'There are three bedrooms. Take your pick,' she offered. 'Have a look around.'

He negotiated the narrow stairs and the low sloping ceiling at the top, and explored the upper floor of the cottage. The bathroom was plain white, with blue curtains at the tiny window and a mirror bordered with shells. The bedrooms were all doubles, with cherrywood *bateaux lits* and prints of seascapes on the wall. He guessed that Zoe would prefer the room at the front of the cottage that overlooked the sea, so he picked the one opposite.

When he came downstairs again, Zoe had opened a bottle of red wine and poured out two glasses. 'There's plenty of hot water, so help yourself if you want a bath.'

'Thanks.' He took the glass of wine from her. 'This place is gorgeous.'

'You wait until tomorrow morning. The sunrises and sunsets around here are incredible. Nothing but sky, the marshes and the sea.'

'You really love it here, don't you?'

Zoe nodded.

'So why didn't you become a doctor around here?'

'I wanted to work in London. I like the buzz of working in a big city hospital,' she explained. 'But here—this is where I can relax, really be me.'

He joined her on the sofa in the living room. 'No TV?' he noted.

'Jay hates it, so she never had a TV set installed—and nobody's been that bothered about getting one.'

'Fine by me. So in summer you have the windows open and listen to birdsong?'

'And in winter you listen to the rain,' she said with a grin. 'But if you get really bored, Jay's got an amazing stock of board-games.' She indicated a cupboard. 'I'm a whiz at Boggle patience. Mainly because nobody will play with me,' she added ruefully.

'I'll challenge you tomorrow—but I'm fine just sitting here right now.' Next to her. And maybe, just maybe, this weekend was going to change both their lives. For the better.

CHAPTER SEVEN

THE sunrise in the morning was everything Zoe had promised it would be. A wide, wide sky with a deep orange ball slowly rising from the palest pink band at the horizon to light the marshes. There had been a sharp frost overnight and mist shimmered just above the surface of the marshes, making the place look otherworldly. Brad kept watching until he heard the clatter of a spoon against china and realised that Zoe was already up and about. He showered swiftly, then went downstairs to join her.

'Good morning.'

'Good morning.' It was the first time he'd seen her in jeans, a pair of faded and well-worn denims. He could imagine how soft the material would feel—and it showed off the curves he'd long suspected. She was wearing yet another of her loose long-sleeved tops, and her hair was still damp from her own shower. No make-up, and she looked like the girl next door. Best-friend material.

Which wasn't how he felt about her.

But he also knew that it was how *she* felt about *him*. So he had to tread carefully.

'Coffee?'

'Thanks.' He took the proffered mug gratefully. Yet another plus point about Zoe Kennedy: she made great coffee.

'I'm just going down to the village to pick up some things for breakfast,' Zoe said. 'It's up to you if you fancy a walk, or you want to stay here and chill out with more coffee and a book.'

'I'll come with you,' he said. 'That sunrise this morning was amazing.'

'I told you it would be.' She smiled. 'That's the thing I miss most in London. The sky. You just don't get the sunrises, the sunsets, or the stars at night. Not like here.'

'You lived around here when you were younger?'

'I spent some of the holidays with Jay.'

She was deliberately not looking at him, and Brad had the feeling that she was hiding something. Though what or why, he had no idea. The only thing he did know was that he had to let her tell him in her own good time. Push her now, and he'd push her away for good.

After coffee, they walked into the village. Zoe bought butter, honey, cheese and free-range eggs from the farm shop, then picked up fresh granary bread from the bakery next door. 'You haven't lived until you've tried this,' she said.

And when she presented him with boiled eggs and toast soldiers, back at the cottage, Brad had to admit she was right. 'Fabulous.'

They walked over the marshes to the shingled beach, where Brad proved that he was better than Zoe at skipping flat pebbles across the surface of the sea.

'That's evidence of a misspent youth,' she teased.

'I grew up by the sea,' Brad said.

'So all that teasing on the ward…are you telling me you actually *do* surf, then?'

'Yep. Though I haven't done it for years. After I qualified, I worked inland.' Lara had never been a big fan of the beach, so they hadn't bothered going at weekends and holidays. He hadn't realised until now that he'd missed the sea, that special scent and taste to the air.

'Paddling and peering into rock pools is more my thing,' Zoe said. 'Actually, it's not a good idea to swim on parts of the coast around here. There's a strong undertow. And the tide comes in really fast. At Brancaster, it's easy to be cut off on one of the sandbanks, and at Wells-next-the-sea there's actually a klaxon to warn you to get back on the right side of the causeway.'

They had lunch at the local pub, then drove into Brandham-on-sea. They parked in the almost deserted car park at the top of the cliffs, then strolled down the narrow path to the town. Brad couldn't resist secretly buying a trilobite for Zoe from the geology shop while she was poring over some of the display cases.

And then they headed for the beach. They walked for miles along the sand and back again, then balanced at the edge of rock pools to see crabs and starfish and mermaids' purses.

Zoe leaned over a bit too far and slipped. A split second before she fell, Brad grabbed her and pulled her against him.

Bad move. Very, very bad move. Because holding her this close made him remember what it had felt like to kiss her. How she'd tasted. The softness of her lips. For a long, long moment his eyes locked with hers. She remembered, too, he could see it in her wide pupils. Desire. Need. And then panic.

Much as he wanted to kiss her again, he let her go. 'OK now?' he asked lightly.

'Thanks for saving me,' she mumbled. 'It isn't much fun getting soaked at this time of year.'

'No.'

She avoided his gaze and tucked her arms protectively round herself. Brad sighed inwardly. He'd hoped that they'd walk together, that their hands would brush together, that she wouldn't object when his fingers tangled

with hers. But it looked as if it would take a little longer
before Zoe would let him hold her hand.

He didn't think she was scared of him. She wouldn't
have invited him here if she didn't at least like him. And
he knew she felt that same pull between them, or she
wouldn't have kissed him back last week. But Zoe was
definitely running scared of something. Somehow, he had
to persuade her to tell him what it was, so he could help
her face it and beat it—just as she'd helped him to face
dealing with eclampsia.

They wandered along the edge of the beach towards the
pier, watching the tide come in. As the sun began to set,
the sky was pale grey and the sea turned almost silver,
with pale orange light reflecting the sunset far out to sea.
'I love it here in winter,' Zoe said. 'Just walking along
and watching the tide come in—and you can't see where
the sea ends and the sky begins.' The sea hissed towards
them, then ebbed out again. In the growing dusk, the pier
was lit up, and they could see the waves rolling in from
the end of it, curling up before sighing onto the beach.
'And the surf, of course.'

'You call *that* surf? It's baby stuff!' Brad said. 'The
waves can't be much taller than you.'

'There's still no way you'd get me out there,' Zoe said
with a shudder.

'Too cold?'

'I go paddling in the middle of winter, remember?' she
teased. 'No. I'm just not into risk-taking.' Not any more.
She'd been there, done that and now she wore the long-
sleeved, high-necked T-shirt.

'It's not that much of a risk if you know what you're
doing,' Brad said. He pointed to the solitary surfer paddling out on his board and then riding the surf. 'Like that
guy. Though it's getting a bit dark to be out there.'

'So you enjoyed surfing?'

'Yes. But in the Atlantic we had real rollers. It's such a high, Zoe. Riding the waves and coming in to land—it's an amazing feeling.'

'I'll take your word for it.'

Brad frowned as they walked along. Zoe had started to relax—but she'd clammed up on him as soon as he'd mentioned surfing. Had she been involved in a surfing accident or something? But before he could try to probe further, Zoe gave a gasp. The surfer had misjudged his balance and had slipped on his board; the wave flung him against the supports of the pier. The sea swept the board away, and the surfer didn't seem to be coming up for air.

There was nobody else around to help. 'He might be trapped. I'll go in.' Brad stripped off his jacket, sweater and boots. 'Have you got a mobile phone on you?'

She nodded.

'Then call an ambulance now.'

'Brad, wait—'

'There isn't time. If he was knocked out or he's caught on the pier supports, hc could drown. Call an ambulance.'

Zoe dug in her handbag and pulled out her mobile phone. She punched in 999 and gave the emergency services all the information they needed while she watched Brad swim towards the pier. He seemed to know exactly what he was doing—swimming diagonally across the current rather than battling against it. Had he done this sort of thing before? She hoped so. He used to be a surfer, she reasoned, so he had to be a strong swimmer. He'd need to be strong, too: cold water sapped a swimmer's stamina.

The seconds dragged by, though at least she could see the surfer again. He didn't appear to be swimming but he was moving with the tide, which meant he wasn't trapped but he *was* unconscious or at least unable to swim. The longer they were in the water, the more likely it was that the surfer—and Brad—would get hypothermia. She tried to remember what she knew about near-drownings. If the surfer had inhaled water, it would be a 'wet' drowning; if he hadn't, but his airway had closed because of spasms induced by water, it would be a 'dry' drowning. Any fluid in the lungs could irritate them, and there was a risk of pneumonia or 'late' drowning, where the fluids accumulated and the victim could die up to three days after immersion.

The important thing was to get the surfer out of the water, then check his breathing, pulse and airway. If he'd arrested, it cut his chances of survival down to one in ten.

But it was going to be hard for Brad to bring him in. She groaned in dismay as she looked at the water and realised there was a rip tide, a fast-flowing run-back current that often formed between groynes on the beach in medium to heavy seas. All the signs were there—the water was brown from sand stirred up at the bottom, the foam on the top spread further than the breaking waves and larger waves broke further out on both sides. She only hoped that Brad could see it from where he was by the pier, and knew to swim through the breaking waves, not try to make it through the rip.

She took off her boots and socks and rolled her jeans up to her knees, ready to help Brad with the swimmer. No matter how strong a swimmer he was, the water couldn't be more than six degrees and the cold would drain him. He'd need her to help him carry the surfer to safety.

To her relief, Brad swam through the waves rather than the rip, keeping the surfer as horizontal as possible. Zoe walked into the sea to meet him. The water was so cold that it almost hurt to walk through it, and the water sucked the sand from under her feet as it ran back again, making it hard for her to keep her balance, but she wasn't going to stop. Not now. Brad needed her. Step by step, she walked in until she was up to her knees in the water and the foam soaked the ends of her rolled-up jeans.

'What the hell do you think you're doing?' Brad yelled hoarsely as he hauled himself to his feet.

'It's easier with two of us.'

'You're taking a hell of a r—'

'We'll argue about it later,' she cut in. 'Let me help you carry him. Is he breathing?'

'Not sure. It's getting heavier out there and there's a rip tide. If I'd tried artificial respiration out there, we'd both have gone under,' Brad said tersely.

And she'd have lost him. Just like Dermot. Leaving a huge hole in her life.

The idea shocked her so much, she almost stumbled.

'Are you all right?' Brad asked.

'Fine.'

'Good. Keep his head to one side,' Brad said, letting her help him with the surfer's weight. 'And keep it lower than his body—that'll stop any water getting from his stomach to his lungs.'

Either Brad had done a long stint in emergency medicine or he'd done some kind of lifesaving course during his surfing days, Zoe thought.

'There's a fair chance he's got hypothermia. Even though he's wearing a wetsuit, the body cools down thirty times faster when immersed in water. And there's the wind chill now.'

She could feel it. Now she was only ankle-deep in water, her bare skin was so cold it was burning.

Together, they carried the surfer up to the sea defences.

Although the tide was still coming in and they might have to move him again, they both knew that they had to assess him first.

'Pale skin, blue lips, no resps, weak pulse and unconscious—he's hypothermic,' Zoe said. 'Did he hit his head on the pier?'

'I can't see a bruise, but that doesn't mean anything right now,' Brad said. 'We'll deal with the hypothermia second. ABCs first.'

'Put your sweater on before you get hypothermia, while I do the ABCs,' she ordered, noticing that he was shivering. 'Airway's clear, still not breathing, thready pulse.'

'Artificial respiration,' Brad said with a sigh.

'I'll do the compressions and you breathe,' Zoe said.

'Remember it's harder if someone's cold and inhaled water. Take it slower than usual—sixty compressions a minute. Keep the compressions four to five centimetres depth,' Brad said.

She nodded and commenced compressions, counting out loud and then pausing so Brad could give two breaths. More compressions, more breaths.

'One, come on. Two, come on! Three, breathe, will you? Four, come on,' Zoe said through gritted teeth. More breaths. More compressions.

'Keep going,' Brad said. 'I'll blow harder. But don't stop.'

More breaths. More compressions.

'Swap,' Brad directed. 'You're getting tired.'

'You've been in the water. I'm stronger than you right now,' she said, continuing the chest compressions. 'Breaths.'

At last, the surfer began to vomit water.

'We're there,' she said, turning him on his side to help the water drain from his lungs.

'Remember, keep his head lower than the body to reduce the risk of reinhaling the water,' Brad said.

'Did you do lifeguard training?'

'Yep. And before you ask, yes, I wore the skimpy red trunks, too. But you tell anyone on Paeds and I'll make your life a misery.'

She grinned, and helped him put the surfer into the recovery position. 'The tide's still coming in. We'll give the ambulance five more minutes—if they're not here by then, we'll need to move him.'

Brad checked the surfer's pulse and respirations. 'OK. Now let's deal with the hypothermia. We'll use my jacket to cover him.'

'And mine. I know rewarming has to be passive, with the heat coming from the core of the body, not externally—but wouldn't body heat help? Say, if I lay next to him?'

'The jackets will do,' Brad said, covering the surfer. 'You could burn him and he'll cool you down very quickly.'

They continued checking the surfer's pulse and respirations, keeping an eye on the approaching tide. Just when they were at the point of carrying the surfer up the steps leading to the promenade, the ambulance arrived. Brad gave the paramedics a quick rundown of what had happened and the patient's condition.

'You ought to go to hospital as well,' Zoe said. 'To warm up.'

Brad shook his head. 'I didn't inhale any water, and I'll be fine as long as I warm up slowly. Let's go home.'

The ambulance drove off and Brad and Zoe headed back up the cliffs to the car park. They walked very quickly, almost at jogging pace, but Brad was still shivering by the time they reached the car.

'You need to get out of those wet clothes,' Zoe said.

'It's only a ten-minute drive.'

'Even so.' She rummaged in the boot of the car and brought out a tartan picnic rug. 'You can use this as a sarong. Just until we get home.' Her lips quirked. 'I promise not to look while you strip off your jeans.'

'You're nearly as wet as I am,' Brad pointed out.

Her rolled-up jeans were wet to mid-thigh and her sweater was wet from where she'd done the chest compressions. 'I've only got one picnic rug—and, anyway, I can't drive wrapped in a blanket. So stop arguing and get your clothes off.'

'Best offer I've had all day,' Brad quipped.

'Funny guy. There's a plastic bag in the boot—put your wet clothes in it.'

She climbed into the driver's seat and waited for Brad to change. At least he'd accepted her argument. But it had been a near thing: she'd seen the set look to his jaw. He'd gone all protective male. But if she'd done what he wanted and stripped off her own wet clothes, he'd have seen a lot more than she wanted him to see. Seen things that would have led to explanations she really, really didn't want to give.

Brad joined her in the car, clad only in the picnic rug.

'What a shame I don't have a camera on me,' she said, pulling out of the car park. 'Nobody's going to believe a word of this. Brad Hutton, superdoc, in a skirt.'

'This stays with the red trunks story. Between you and me. Not a word to anyone—and that includes Holly and Judith.'

'They don't know what they've missed,' she teased. But she was glad she was driving. Teasing apart, Brad had a gorgeous body, and the rug did very little to hide it. Broad shoulders, a washboard-flat abdomen and strong, well-shaped legs. She could imagine him wearing a kilt and a dinner-jacket—he'd look amazing. Or wrapped only in a towel, his skin damp and warm from a shower rather than wet and clammy from the cold sea. And the picture was so vivid she had to bite back a moan of desire.

Focus, she reminded herself sharply. Focus. This can't go any further than your imagination. Hands off.

If only things were different. If only she'd said no to Dermot, that mad, crazy night. If only…

Brad watched Zoe surreptitiously. That noise she'd just made had sounded suspiciously like a moan. An appreciative moan. He could see her nipples, but that was surely a physiological reaction to cold, because her sweater was wet. Or was she, like him, thinking about how good they'd be together?

It was just as well he was wearing the blanket, not her. Apart from the fact that seeing her wrapped in nothing but a blanket might have blown his self-control sky-high, right now it was covering a potentially embarrassing situation.

He had to get himself back under control before they reached the cottage. Before he begged her to unwrap the blanket and warm him up with her body heat. Before he scared her away, for good.

CHAPTER EIGHT

'GO AND warm up in the shower. Now,' Zoe said as she opened the front door. 'No arguments or trying to be a gentleman. You were immersed and I wasn't.'

Wearing nothing but a picnic blanket, Brad was in no position to argue. And, anyway, he knew she was right. He gave in and headed for the shower. He kept the water tepid, letting his body warm up gradually, then changed into clean jeans and a sweater.

When he came downstairs, Zoe had already changed, also into a pair of dry jeans and a sweater. 'Here,' she said, handing him a mug. 'Sit down and get that into you.'

'What's this?'

'Hot, sweet tea. It tastes revolting, but it'll do you good.'

He sat down at the pine table and took a sip, then grimaced. 'Zoe, this is gross.'

'But you need it. Drink it,' she ordered. 'And I'll know if you pour it down the sink while I'm in the shower.'

'Hurricane Zoe,' he teased.

'You'd better believe it,' she teased back as she walked upstairs.

He did. Because she'd spun his world round completely. He began to hum the chorus of Neil Young's 'Like A Hurricane'.

'I heard that!' she called back down the stairs.

This was the Zoe he loved. Warm and laughing and...

Loved?

It was just as well he was sitting down. Loved. He was

in love with Zoe Kennedy. How had that happened? When? He really wasn't sure. He'd been in tune with her at work right from the very start. He'd noted the way she looked after her patients, talking to them and spending time with their parents, too, warm and caring. He'd appreciated the way she'd drawn him into the hospital life through the fund-raiser and had made sure he felt part of London City General. She'd cooked brownies for him. She'd let him pour his heart out when he'd stopped coping and his world had finally fallen apart. She'd made him feel again.

But it wasn't simple gratitude or liking or even lust he felt for her. It was something very different. Body and heart and soul, Brad loved her. Loved her bravery, the way she'd walked through the edge of the rip tide to help him rescue the surfer. Loved her mouth, the tempting curve that had made him want to kiss her—that made him want to do it even more now he'd kissed her and felt her response. Loved the smile in her beautiful brown eyes.

Yet Zoe had been at pains to make it clear she'd invited him here as her friend, nothing more. Despite the fact that she'd kissed him back. Why was she keeping him at arm's length? And was he the one who could heal the sadness he instinctively knew she kept hidden, the way she'd shown him how to heal his own hurts?

His thoughts were still raging when she came downstairs again, smelling sweet and fresh from the shower.

'Penny for them,' she said lightly.

'Trust me, you wouldn't want to know my thoughts right now.'

She glanced at his almost full mug. 'OK. So the tea's vile. But it's supposed to be good for shock.'

Not the kind of shock *he'd* just had.

At his continuing silence, she groaned. 'All right. I won't make you drink it. I've got a better idea.'

So had he. Not that he could suggest it to her. 'Such as?'

'Fish and chips, wine and your chocolates.'

'Sounds good.'

She drove them back to Brandham, where they bought fish and chips, but when they returned to the cottage and Zoe tried turning the light on, she growled in frustration. 'Rats. A fuse must have blown.'

'Got a torch and a spare fuse? I'll fix it for you,' Brad offered.

'Thanks. That fuse box hates me.' She handed him the carrier bag of fish and chips. 'Hold these and I'll get them.' She fumbled through the kitchen, and a few moments later Brad saw a torch beam. Then he heard her exclaim in annoyance. 'I don't *believe* this! I always make sure there's a spare. I bet it blew last time Ned was here and he forgot to get another one.'

'Ned?'

'My cousin. Otherwise known as the family scatter-brain. Oh, great. The local shops are shut now and the nearest DIY warehouse place is probably in Norwich.' She glanced at her watch. 'It'll be closed by the time we get there.'

'Can we get a fuse tomorrow?'

'Yeah.' He could hear her rummaging in a cupboard. 'Well, at least he hasn't used all the candles.' Further rummaging. 'Or the matches. Looks like we'll be eating by candlelight tonight.'

'That's fine.' Brad closed the door behind him as she lit a couple of candles and put them in the middle of the pine table. 'Actually, this is rather nice.'

'You might not say that in a couple of hours' time. No

electric means no heat, as well as no light. And no hot water either.'

'We'll survive.' He put the food on the plates while Zoe cut some bread and poured the wine.

'Well, cheers,' she said, sitting opposite him.

'Cheers.' He clinked his glass against hers, then ate his fish and chips appreciatively. 'These are good. I hadn't realised how hungry I was.'

'Best chips for miles,' Zoe told him.

When their plates were clear, Zoe eyed him speculatively. 'The water'll be cold so we can't wash up until tomorrow. I seem to remember you promising me a game of Boggle.'

'By candlelight. Winner of each game gets a chocolate.'

Zoe took the game from the cupboard and set it between them, together with the box of chocolates. 'You'll regret saying that. These are mine, all mine,' she teased.

'Don't count your chickens,' Brad advised her. And proceeded to beat her, three games in a row.

'Mine,' he said, taking his third chocolate.

'Not fair. He sings, he saves lives *and* he doesn't warn me he's a Boggle champ.' Zoe sighed theatrically.

'OK. I'll take pity on you and share.' He bit precisely half the chocolate and held the other half to her lips.

Was it his imagination, a trick of the candlelight or were her pupils just that little bit wider than they should be? He'd have bet money that his own were when her lips touched his fingers for just a second. Because he could imagine that sweet mouth on other parts of his body. And that distracted him so much that he lost the next game.

Zoe crowed, 'Victory at last!' Then she chose a chocolate, deliberately ate half of it and held the other half out to his lips. 'Consolation prize.'

Brad would have preferred a kiss, but knew that now was the wrong time to ask. Instead, he let her feed him the chocolate, and hoped his eyes would say it all for him.

The rest of the chocolates went the same way—the winner fed the loser precisely half the chocolate. By the time they'd finished, Brad was aching in frustration, wanting her but not daring to push her too far, too soon.

She stretched, yawned, then stretched again. 'It must be the sea air—I'm shattered. I'm going to turn in now but you're welcome to stay up.'

'And play Boggle solitaire?' he teased. 'No. I'm tired, too.'

'Right.' She extinguished all the candles bar one, which she used to light their way upstairs. With the heating not working, the cottage had cooled down and Zoe's teeth were chattering by the time they got to the top of the stairs.

The words came out before he could stop them. 'Zoe, you're shivering. We've both been soaked in the sea, we're both cold and there's no heating. You know what would be the sensible thing to do, don't you?'

'What?'

'Share a duvet.' Her back went rigid and he could have kicked himself. Time to backtrack. 'Purely for extra body warmth,' he added.

Extra body warmth. He was right: it was freezing and she could do with the extra heat. But sharing a bed with Brad would be torture and paradise at the same time.

What was she going to do? If she said yes, she'd have to exercise major self-control because she couldn't possibly touch him in the way she wanted to. But if she said no, she'd have to explain why she didn't want to share a bed with him. And that explanation would lead to other, much more difficult explanations.

Hoping her voice didn't sound as squeaky to him as it did to her own ears, she said, 'OK. Meet you in your bed in ten minutes. Get your PJs on.'

He coughed. 'There's a small problem.'

'What?'

'I don't wear pyjamas.'

Zoe's knees started to quiver at the idea of Brad sleeping in the nude. Next to her. Keeping her warm. 'Improvise,' she said, and fled into her own room before he could make a comment about how wobbly her voice sounded.

When she walked into his room, ten minutes later, it was without the candle.

'No light?' he asked.

'For safety's sake,' she said. Though it was a feeble excuse. She just didn't want him to see her blushing.

'I'm decent, just in case you were worried.' His voice held a hint of amusement.

Worried? She was petrified!

'Jockey shorts and a T-shirt.' He paused, and when she still made no move towards the bed, his voice softened. 'Relax, Zoe. We're friends, yes?'

'Yes.'

'And we're doing this to conserve body heat.'

'Yes.'

'I'm not going to leap on you. You're perfectly safe.'

Was she?

For that matter, was *he*? Her self-control wasn't that good. Right now, she was having third, fourth and fifth thoughts about this.

'Zo, I'm cold. So are you. Come here.'

That husky, almost pleading note in his voice undid her. She went.

It was the first time she'd shared a bed with a man in ten years. Then, it had been a complete disaster. Now...

No, this was different. They were just going to *sleep* together. They weren't planning to have sex. Brad wasn't going to see her. Wasn't going to touch her. Wasn't going to discover the side of Zoe Kennedy that nobody at London City General knew about.

And it felt good to be wrapped in his arms. To have her face resting against his chest and her arm loosely round his waist, while he held her close to him. To breathe in his clean, masculine scent. To feel safe, knowing that Brad would never hurt her. It felt so good that she almost cried. She snuggled closer, willing the tears to stay back.

It was the first time Brad had shared a bed with a woman since Lara's death. But Zoe wasn't just any woman. She'd exploded into his heart. And having her in his arms right now was sweet, sublime torture.

He could hear the regular rise and fall of her breathing. Asleep. So she'd relaxed that much with him. Good.

Then she moved closer to him in her sleep, and he couldn't resist dropping a kiss on the top of her head. Except, once he'd started kissing her, he couldn't make himself stop. Her eyebrow was next. The tip of her nose. The curve of her neck.

Zoe was dreaming. Dreaming that Brad was holding her, stroking her back, teasing her with a trail of kisses along her neck, as far as he could reach under her pyjamas. She moved against him and tipped her head back, murmuring a demand for a proper kiss. And she got one. Soft and sweet, asking rather than demanding. And when she responded, he deepened the kiss, touching his tongue to hers, inciting her to kiss him back.

'Zoe, my beautiful Zoe,' he murmured as he broke the kiss. 'I want you. I want to make love with you.'

'Yes.' The word was a husky groan.

He slid his hand under the hem of her pyjama top. 'I want to touch you, Zoe. I want to taste you.' He undid the lowest button.

Panic lanced through her. 'No!'

His hand stilled. 'OK.'

'I didn't mean ''no'' no,' she mumbled. She didn't want him to stop now. But she didn't want his hands to go any further under her pyjama top. Didn't want to feel his body stiffen with shock and revulsion when he discovered her scars. 'Too cold to take my top off.' It wasn't a lie, just not the whole truth. She just hoped it would sidetrack him.

His hand skimmed across her abdomen. 'I see.' He nuzzled her neck. 'So it wasn't a no, then?'

'No.' She slid one leg over his and tilted her hips against him. The pressure felt good, but it wasn't enough. She wanted more.

'You want me as much as I want you?'

'I…' Her throat dried. 'I want you.' Words she'd never imagined she'd ever say again.

'My beautiful Zoe,' he breathed, and lifted her hips. Her pyjama bottoms were gone as if by magic. And then he slid one hand between her thighs.

She gave a hiss of pleasure as his thumb found just the right spot. *'Yes.'*

And then he was touching her, sliding a finger into her warm wet heat, stirring her desire until she bucked her hips towards him and dug her fingers into his shoulders, wanting more.

'Touch me,' he demanded, his voice a ragged whisper. 'Touch me, Zoe.'

Almost shyly, she stroked his hip. Let her hand drift underneath the edge of the boxers, and discovered just how hard and tight his buttocks were—they felt even better than they'd looked in his faded jeans. And then she grew bolder, curled her fingers round him and smiled in satisfaction when he gasped.

'You asked for it,' she reminded him.

'Mmm, and I got exactly what I wanted.' His voice was low and deep and sexy as hell. 'Except I want more.' He paused. 'I want you, Zoe. I need to be inside you. Right now.'

The huskiness in his voice told her how much he desired her, and a thrill ran down her spine. To be wanted that much by a man as gorgeous as Brad Hutton... And she wanted him, too. Just as badly. 'Yes,' she said.

He eased her onto her back. Knelt between her thighs. Kissed her, teased her with his fingers until she was at the point of begging him to do it right now. And then slowly, slowly he entered her.

Then Zoe realised she *wasn't* dreaming. Brad really was making love with her. This was the first time she'd made love since Dermot and she'd forgotten how good it could be, the feel of the man she loved filling her so completely.

Loved? No. She couldn't be in love with Brad. Impossible. She'd kept true to her promise never to let anyone that close again. But he was here with her, right now, in the wide double bed. Making love with her. Her legs were wrapped around his waist, he was kissing her and his body was doing incredible things to hers. Making her feel things she'd forgotten how to feel, the way her climax rose and rose and rose like a tidal wave, then came crashing around her and swept her away.

When she came back to earth, Brad was kissing her and she was wrapped tightly in his arms.

'You were hyperventilating,' he said as he broke the kiss. 'I had to do something.'

'Mmm.' She stroked his face. 'That was…'

'I know. Me, too.' He turned his head and pressed a kiss into her palm. 'Shh. Let me hold you. Go to sleep.'

'Yeah.' If you could sleep when your smile was a mile wide.

Later that night, she woke to find herself still wrapped in Brad's arms. Her cheek was pillowed against his chest and the scattering of blond hair tickled her skin. He'd looked like a sea god when he'd been striding out of the ocean, carrying the surfer. Tall and blond and muscular and gorgeous. Who'd have guessed his skin would be so soft? she thought dreamily, letting her hand splay against his back. She could imagine him as a merman, king of the seas, a crown on his head and seaweed strewn through his hair. Though, of course, his hair would be long. And his soft skin would turn into the even softer scales of a merman when her hand drifted down over his hip.

Brad was dimly aware of a soft, soft hand stroking his skin. Exploring his back. Splaying over his side. Stroking his hip.

Zoe.

He was wide awake in an instant. It wasn't a dream. He was at the cottage, sharing a bed with Zoe. She'd given herself wholeheartedly to him. And, right now, she clearly thought he was asleep and she was exploring.

Exploring was just fine by him.

He gave what he hoped sounded like a dreamy murmur and shifted onto his back. Her tentative exploration grew a little bolder. And bolder still. And then his heart nearly stopped as he felt her kiss his chest. Felt her hair tickling his abdomen as she moved lower, lower still. And it was his turn to hyperventilate as she used her mouth exactly where he wanted it most.

'Oh, Zoe,' he murmured, stroking her hair and arching his hips. 'Oh, yes.'

He felt rather than saw the wicked grin on her mouth as she kissed all the way back up his body. And then he lifted her onto him and jammed his mouth onto hers, kissing her deeply. This was a perfect moment, one he'd remember for ever: joined as one with the woman he loved. Feeling her body ripple around his. Zoe's scent and touch and taste filling his senses. Drowning in an ocean of bliss.

As he climaxed, he called out her name, heard her answering cry, and then she collapsed onto him. He could feel her heart beating, just as hard and fast as his own. She was still wearing her pyjama top, the cotton the only barrier to stop him feeling the softness of her skin against his, but unless he moved her he couldn't undo the buttons or pull it over her head. And no way was he going to move right now, because she was exactly where he wanted her to be. In his arms.

Zoe couldn't quite believe what she'd just done. But she had no regrets. She'd wanted to touch Brad—to taste him—intimately. Feel the power surging through his body as his desire rose. And he'd reacted beyond her wildest dreams.

She knew that it couldn't continue—how could it, once he found out the truth about her?—but she wanted tonight. Something to remember for the rest of her life. A good memory to take away some of the bad. And lying here on top of him, her head buried in his shoulder and his lips against her hair and his arms wrapped around her—this was perfect. A perfect moment, a perfect memory.

As she drifted off to sleep, she thought she heard him

say, 'I love you.' But his voice was so quiet, she wasn't sure which side of sleep it belonged to: dream or waking. Dream, she decided.

The best dream of all.

CHAPTER NINE

THE next morning, Zoe woke and her dreams faded fast. She was lying on her side and there was a warm body curved around hers. Brad's. His face was against her neck and she could feel the regularity of his breathing, which told her that he was still sound asleep. His right arm was curved under her pyjama jacket, and his hand was flat against her abdomen. Just a couple of handspans away from revealing a lot more than she wanted him to know.

How could she have been so stupid? She'd made love with him. More than once. She'd let him through every single defence. Which left her with two choices—tell him the truth or tell him they had to stop. Now.

Telling him the truth was a risk. A huge risk. She knew Brad wouldn't reject her the way her college boyfriend had done—the boyfriend whose name she couldn't even remember now. He'd been little more than a kid himself, immature and selfish, and he hadn't meant to hurt her so badly. But Brad was an adult. An honourable man. He might feel he had to stay with her out of duty. Out of *pity*. And she really couldn't bear that.

As for telling him they had to stop—that would hurt. Badly. But knowing that he was only with her because he felt sorry for her... That would be far worse. It would break her heart. And she knew she'd never, ever get over that.

Put like that, she didn't have a choice. Badly hurt or broken heart. Either way, she lost.

Slowly, very gently she moved his hand. Wriggled

away from him. Left their bed without disturbing him. And went back to her own room to prepare herself for what she knew was the right thing to do.

Brad knew something was wrong when he woke up to find himself alone in bed. Zoe's pillow was cold enough to tell him that she'd been gone for some time. She'd gone, rather than staying in bed with him and waiting for him to wake up. Which meant…what?

She'd been running scared the first time he'd kissed her. And on the beach, when he'd stopped her slipping on the rocks. Someone had obviously hurt her very badly in the past. But last night she'd trusted him enough to make love with him. To offer him the ultimate intimacy. She'd been his, completely.

So what had changed since last night?

He discovered just how badly wrong things were when he went downstairs, wearing just his boxers and a T-shirt. Zoe was sitting at the kitchen table, fully dressed, and there was a brittleness to her smile that turned his insides to ice.

'Good morning,' he said cautiously.

'Good morning.' She smiled again. And then she plunged the knife into his heart. 'About last night. I think we should forget about it.'

'Forget about it?' His jaw dropped. 'Zoe, we made love.'

'We had sex,' she corrected.

It had been more than just sex, and they both knew it. But her chin was tilted up to maximum stubbornness level. This wasn't an argument he could win.

'You're a man, I'm a woman,' she continued.

Yeah. He knew that.

'And last night…was just because we were both a bit on edge. Both full of adrenaline. Because of the rescue.'

'Because of the rescue,' he repeated. Was she crazy? Didn't she have any idea how he felt about her? Hadn't she heard him tell her that he loved her?

Or didn't that matter to her at all?

'I rang the hospital this morning. Ted's fine.'

'Ted?' Brad was mystified. Who was Ted?

'The surfer. They're keeping him in for another forty-eight hours' obs, just to be on the safe side. You know, in case of "late drowning".'

'Right.' She was babbling again. Talking to keep their minds off the real problem: last night.

'Anyway. What I'm trying to say is that we shouldn't confuse things because of last night. I think we should just forget about it and go back to being friends.'

Forget about it? She honestly expected him to forget something that intense, that special?

'If we don't, it could cause all kinds of problems at work.'

No, it wouldn't. But he didn't waste his breath arguing with her. There was a much more important issue at stake. 'What about the consequences?' he asked softly.

Her eyes narrowed. 'Consequences?'

'We didn't use protection.' Because he hadn't been thinking straight. And neither had she.

Her mouth tightened. 'I'm not in the habit of sleeping around.'

'Neither am I.' He sighed, guessing what she'd immediately assumed. 'And that wasn't what I meant. I was thinking something more long term. Like an event, say, nine months from now.'

Her face drained of colour. 'A baby? No.'

'How can you be so sure? Unless you're on the Pill—and even then that isn't one hundred per cent guaranteed.'

'I just know, OK?' she said through gritted teeth.

'And supposing you're wrong? Supposing we made a baby last night, Zoe?'

She took a deep breath. 'You're a doctor. So you know the chances of my conceiving are one in four—and that's assuming that we made love around the midpoint of my cycle. I'm not at the midpoint. Plus I'm nearly thirty, which means my fertility levels are lower than a twenty-year-old's. So it's unlikely I'm pregnant.'

'*Unlikely*, yes. But not impossible.' He looked her straight in the eye. 'Which means that right now you could be carrying my baby.'

'If I am...' She lowered her gaze so he couldn't tell what she was thinking. 'Then we'll work something out.'

'Like what?' Surely she wouldn't consider a termination?

'There's no point in stressing about something that's highly unlikely and we won't know about for another three weeks in any case.' She sighed. ''Look, I can take the morning-after pill when we get back to London.' She folded her arms and looked him in the eye again. 'I need to get a fuse, and a spare. I'll be back soon.'

So she didn't even want him to go with her. Worse and worse. If he pushed, this whole thing would blow up in his face. He bit back the urge to pull her into his arms and kiss her until she was thinking straight again. Instead, he did the sensible thing. 'I'll pack while you're away. Then I'll fix the fuse while you pack.'

'Fine.'

Walking away from Brad was one of the hardest things Zoe had ever done. But Brad had known enough heart-

ache in his life. He'd lost his wife and his baby. The least
she could do for him was give him the chance to find
someone else. Someone who wasn't damaged goods.

And if she was carrying his baby...

No. The chances were too small. She wasn't going to
torture herself by imagining what it would be like. To feel
her belly swell and grow round, to feel that tiny fluttering
as if someone was blowing bubbles inside her when the
baby first moved, to see a foot or a hand pushing out and
travelling from one side of her abdomen to the other as
the baby turned over.

She wasn't cut out for babies or marriage. Those
dreams had died thirteen years ago, along with Dermot.
She was Zoe Kennedy, a hard-working paediatric registrar
on the fast track to a consultancy. And she'd better remember it.

When she returned to the cottage with the fuses, some
more candles and matches, Brad tackled the fuse box
while she packed. She stripped the beds and put the washing in the machine, then showered while he waited po-
litely for her. 'Want to go for a last walk along the beach
while the washing's doing?' she asked.

'Why not?'

At least he wasn't pushing her, she thought with relief.
Maybe they could salvage some sort of friendship from
this mess.

Zoe kept her arms folded as they walked over the shingle
beach. Brad watched her surreptitiously. After last night,
he'd imagined them walking along the beach together
hand in hand, or with their arms wrapped around each
other. Just like lovers did.

And they'd been lovers. There was no doubt about it.

Zoe had matched him kiss for kiss, sigh for sigh, climax for climax.

But right now she was completely unreachable. She wasn't going to give him even the tiniest clue about what had set her running scared again. Clearly she'd been hurt badly by a previous lover. Had he said or done something last night to remind her of past hurt? Or maybe it was something he *hadn't* said or done.

Not that he could ask her. She'd made it clear that she didn't want to discuss last night any further.

All she was offering was friendship. So he'd take it. And maybe he'd be able to teach her to let go, and give him the relationship they both wanted.

Lunch was a silent affair, the remainder of the bread and cheese she'd bought the day before. When the bedding was dry, they remade the beds. Not together, though Brad knew that it was for the best. His self-control wasn't that brilliant. And if she'd helped him replace the cover on the duvet they'd shared last night, he might not have been able to stop himself tumbling her onto the bed and kissing her until neither of them could think straight.

Zoe drove them back to London. Again, she was virtually silent and Brad spent his time looking out of the window, watching the scenery it had been too dark to see on the Friday night. Gentle folds and hills, wide skies and huge pine forests gave way to the motorway, and then they were back in the city.

She parked on the road just outside his flat.

Hell. He couldn't let her go like this. This wasn't even friendship. If he left this until tomorrow, she'd build a wall between them so high and deep he'd never be able to scale it.

'Thanks for dropping me off. Um, would you like to come in for a coffee?'

Yes. But if she did, it wouldn't stop at coffee. Spending the last two and a half hours in a car with him had tested her control to its limit. She gave him her best fake smile. 'Thanks for the offer, but I'd better say no. I've got some papers I ought to catch up on.'

'Fair enough.' He dug in his pocket. 'By the way, I got this for you. I don't think it was hurt by the sea.'

Mystified, she took the small box from him. One corner had a salty watermark across it, and the cardboard there was clearly weaker than the rest of the box.

It didn't *look* like the kind of box that held jewellery, and it was definitely bigger than the velvet-covered sort of box that usually held a ring. Not that Brad would buy her a ring anyway. So what was it? Earrings? Hardly. She didn't have pierced ears. The box was too small to hold a bangle. So…

'Don't open it now,' he said, before she could take the lid off. 'Later. But it's a thank-you for the weekend. For taking me to a place that's special to you.' He paused. 'And for being a good friend.'

A good friend. The words she'd wanted him to say. She'd got exactly what she'd wished for. So why did it hurt so much?

She didn't dare look him in the eye. And she knew her voice wasn't quite steady when she said, 'Pleasure. And thanks for the gift.' Hopefully he'd put it down to tiredness after the drive.

'See you tomorrow,' he said.

Oh, yes. And by then she'd be back to being happy, smiley, Hurricane Zoe. The persona she'd crafted for herself thirteen years ago. 'See you tomorrow,' she said, and drove home.

Determined to be sensible, she unpacked and loaded the washing machine with her clothes and towels from the weekend. But all the time she was thinking about the little box. The watermark and his comment about the sea meant it must have been in his jeans pocket when he'd rescued the surfer, so he'd obviously bought whatever it was in Brandham.

Unable to resist any longer, she opened the box, and gasped. He'd bought her a fossil. Not just any fossil: a trilobite. An early arthropod with a hard shell, around three centimetres long, with a long central or axial lobe flanked by two pleural lobes.

Exactly the kind of fossil she'd always wanted to find on the beach.

It was a superb specimen. She ran her fingers gently over the thorax, noting how clear the divisions were. Brad must have seen her lingering over the display case, guessed how much she wanted one, and he'd bought one for her without her even noticing. It was exactly the sort of gesture her perfect man would make.

And Brad was perfect for her. Or he would have been, if she hadn't been damaged goods.

The back of her throat felt tight. If only she'd never met Dermot. No—that was unfair. They'd had good times and she didn't regret a moment of loving Dermot. But if only she'd been sensible when she was sixteen.

If only she'd been sensible last night.

A tear oozed down her cheek and she brushed it away. She wasn't going to cry. Not over Brad. She'd cried herself out all those years ago. And there was no point in wishing for something she knew she couldn't have.

The following morning, Zoe was relieved to find that she was on the paediatric assessment unit and Brad was on the ward. Hopefully, by the time their paths crossed, she'd be able to face him with professional detachment.

Most of the morning's cases weren't anything out of the ordinary, but then Holly rang up from the emergency department. 'Zo, we've got a four-year-old here I think needs admitting. He's got stridor but I don't think it's croup. Can you come and take a look?'

'Sure.' Zoe went straight down to the emergency department. 'How are things with Daniel?' she asked Holly as her friend led her through to the cubicles.

Holly sighed. 'The usual. He's full of the sorries, and it'll last for six months before he does it all over again and big sis has to go and haul him out of the mess he's made.' She wrinkled her nose. 'I know it's a long-term thing, but sometimes I wish I could speed it up a bit. Inject some common sense into him.' She shook herself. 'Enough of my problems. How was your weekend? Did you go to Marsh End?'

'Yeah. The sea air blew away the cobwebs.'

'It's not as much fun on your own, though. Sorry I let you down. Jude's feeling guilty, too. We both owe you lots of ice-cream.'

Zoe smiled. 'No, you don't. I wasn't on my own.'

'No?'

'I took Brad with me.' Zoe knew she'd made a mistake the moment the words were out, because Holly's eyebrows rose.

'Did you have a nice time?' Holly enquired, her tone neutral but her face full of interest.

'Yes. And, before you start getting any ideas, we're just friends,' Zoe informed her. 'He was an honorary girlie for the weekend.'

Holly's smile said she didn't believe a word of it, and Zoe sighed inwardly. 'I'm as married to my career as you are, so don't start. Where's my four-year-old, then?'

'Here.' Holly pulled the curtain back and introduced

them quickly. 'Zoe, this is George Thurston, and this is Lena, his mum. Lena, this is Zoe Kennedy, our paediatric registrar. She's brilliant with kids.'

Zoe shook Lena's hand, then sat down beside the little boy. 'Hello, George,' she said softly, stroking the little boy's hand.

George tried to speak but started coughing. The barking sound was very similar to the cough caused by croup—but when he started to breathe in, Zoe noted the high-pitched crowing sound of inspiratory stridor. His nostrils were flared; she checked his temperature. Way too high. 'Has he had a sore throat at all?' she asked Lena.

'For a couple of days. I thought it was just a cold—you know what the bugs are like this time of year,' Lena said. 'Half his class are off school with a virus. But then this horrible cough started. I've tried putting him in a steamy bathroom but it didn't make any difference, and my GP told me to bring him straight here.'

Zoe nodded. 'If he's not responding to a humid atmosphere, it's probably not croup.'

'What is it?'

'I'll need to do some tests but I think it could be something called bacterial tracheitis. If it is, we can clear it with antibiotics, but I'd like to keep an eye on him for a couple of days. George, I'm just going to listen to your chest, sweetheart. Can you lift your T-shirt for me?'

There was nothing abnormal on the stethoscope, but Zoe noticed the muscles between his ribs pulling in when he tried to breathe. 'Well done, sweetheart. Now, I'm just going to put something into your nose, very quickly, to take a sample for a test.' When the lab ran the culture, they'd probably find *Staphylococcus aureus*; but there were half a dozen other potential culprits, and she needed to know which one so she could give him the right anti-biotic.

'Well done,' she said again when she'd finished. 'I'm just going to take a blood sample, too. Then I'm going to take you to X-Ray, where they'll take a special photograph of your throat for me, and then we'll go upstairs to my ward and settle you in, OK? And I'm going to give you one of my special bravery certificates.'

The little boy nodded, clearly feeling too ill to say much.

Zoe capped her mucus sample, then did the blood sample and went to find Holly. 'Holls, can you get someone to run these to the lab for me, please? Ask them to send the results straight to Paeds.'

'Sure.' Holly took the sample. 'Let me know how George gets on, OK?'

'I'll ring you later,' Zoe promised. Though she knew that her best friend wanted to know more than just about the little boy—she wanted to know about the weekend with Brad. Zoe had a feeling that Holly would enlist Judith's help, too, and she'd be dragged to Giovanni's tonight and threatened with no ice-cream or latte until she spilled the beans. All of them.

After the X-ray, she took Lena and George up to the ward.

'So this bacterial tracky-wotsit—is it very common?' Lena asked.

'Not that common,' Zoe admitted. 'Ninety-eight per cent of children who cough like this have viral croup. Tracheitis mimics it, and it usually follows a cough or cold. We only know it's tracheitis when the cough doesn't respond to the usual croup treatments—such as steamy bathrooms.'

'How did he get it?'

'It's usually caused by a bacterium called *Staphylococcus aureus*. The infection makes his larynx, trachea and airways swell, and there's a fair amount of sticky mucus, so that's what's causing the cough and breathing problems. I'll put him on antibiotics, though I might need to change them depending on what the results from the lab say. Is he allergic to penicillin at all, or is there a history of allergy in the family?'

'No.'

'That's good,' Zoe said with a smile. 'There's a chance he'll get a little bit worse before he starts to get better—when the mucus loosens, it sometimes blocks the airways, so we may need to help him breathe. That means we might have to put a tube down his throat—it'll look scary, but it will help him. And he should be well on the mend within the next five days.'

'He's not going to die, then?'

Lena looked anxious, and Zoe decided not to mention the other complications just yet. As long as they kept a close watch on him, they'd be able to avoid airway obstruction, where the breathing stopped and then the heartbeat stopped. As for bacterial pneumonia, toxic shock or septicaemia, she'd make sure he was in the care of one of the most experienced nurses, who'd be able to spot the signs and call her straight away. 'We'll keep a very close eye on him. I'll ask Erin to look after him for you—she's a very experienced paediatric nurse and George will be in good hands.'

She gave the little boy antibiotics, settled him into bed, then introduced him and Lena to Erin before chasing up the blood gas and X-ray results. As she suspected, the blood gases showed that George's oxygen saturation was down, which meant he'd need oxygen support. She was checking the films on the light box when she realised that someone was behind her.

Brad.

She knew it was him without even hearing his voice or turning round to look at him. Only Brad gave her goosebumps and made her heart rate speed up.

And we're just friends, remember? she told herself. She pinned a bright smile on her face. 'Hi. Had a good morning?'

'Reasonable. How about you?'

'Usual PAU.'

He nodded. 'What have you got there?'

'Suspected bacterial tracheitis.' She studied the film. 'His epiglottis is normal, so at least it's not epiglottitis. But his airway's narrowed—I'll ask Erin to keep a very close eye on him.'

'Have you done a laryngotracheobronchoscopy?'

Zoe shook her head. 'He's distressed enough without having a tube shoved down his throat. I'm pretty sure if we looked we'd see tracheal secretions.'

'The procedure can help ease the child's breathing by stripping the purulent membranes out,' Brad reminded her. 'Have you done a culture?'

'Yep. It's at the lab. My money's on *Staph aureus*.'

'And you're giving him IV penicillin?'

'For the time being—when the culture's back, depending on the results, I might need to give him a cephalosporin. I'm going to put him on oxygen. And just cross your fingers for me that I don't need to intubate him.' She grimaced. 'That's one of my least favourite jobs.'

'Just remember to use a tube half to one size smaller than usual, to minimise trauma to his throat,' Brad said. 'Or, if I'm around, give me a yell.'

'You'd do it for me?'

'That's what consultants are for. To do the nasty stuff.'

Which was why she really ought to do it herself. How could she possibly expect promotion if she couldn't do the job?

Her thoughts must have shown on her face, because he touched her cheek lightly. 'Don't beat yourself up, Zo. Nobody's perfect.'

His touch nearly undid her, reminding her of how good it felt to be in his arms. To be making love with him. But she toughed it out. 'I'm working on it.'

Though when George's breathing worsened, a couple of hours later, and she had to do the intubation, she was relieved when Brad walked into the bay.

'I was an airway specialist in California. Sometimes you learn as much by watching as by doing,' he said softly, and winked at her.

A wink that would have sent her knees weak, if she hadn't been concentrating a hundred per cent on her job.

'I need you to keep him calm for me,' he said, still using that soft, gentle voice. She sat at the little boy's bedside, holding his hands in one of hers and stroking his forehead, speaking calmly to him as Brad did the intubation.

When George was settled again and she'd explained to Lena what they were doing, she went to Brad's office and knocked on the door.

'I just wanted to thank you,' she said. 'For helping me out.'

'Any time. That's what I'm here for.'

Yes. And everybody on the ward could depend on Brad's support and knowledge and care. As a doctor, he was faultless.

And as a person… If only she dared let herself trust him. She had a feeling he'd be just as dependable as he was at work. But she really, really couldn't take the risk. Just in case.

'And, um, thanks for my trilobite,' she said.

'I thought you'd like it.'

Those blue, blue eyes held another message. But right now she didn't dare read it. 'I'll catch you later. Better check on my patients,' she said, knowing that she was being a complete coward but not knowing what else to do.

CHAPTER TEN

'SO YOU went to Marsh End with Brad. And?' Holly asked, folding her arms and looking intently at Zoe.

'And we walked by the sea, he rescued a surfer from drowning and we came home yesterday,' Zoe said, hoping that would be enough to satisfy Holly's curiosity and stop her probing for the truth about Zoe's relationship with Brad.

'Hang on. He did a beach rescue?' Judith asked. 'So all that surf-boy stuff is true, then?'

'Don't say a word, not a single word, to anyone at London City General,' Zoe warned, 'or I'll be cat food!'

'I can just see him in a pair of skimpy red trunks,' Judith said with a grin. 'Sex on legs.'

Zoe ignored the little stab of jealousy. If her best friend fancied Brad, who was she to stand in Jude's way? Jude at least could offer him a future. She couldn't.

'So you had a good weekend together,' Holly said.

'As *friends*,' Zoe insisted.

Judith sighed. 'What's the real problem, Zo?'

'There isn't a problem. Look, you're both concentrating on your careers. Why can't I do the same with mine?' Zoe protested.

'Because you don't need to work at it in the same way that we do,' Judith said. 'You got the highest marks in the university's history in your finals.'

'That's academic,' Zoe muttered.

Holly chuckled. 'Nice pun, even though you didn't intend it. Seriously, Zo, I don't understand why you're holding back. He's lovely. He likes you a lot. You like him, too, even if you're not going to admit it—I can tell.'

'Me, too,' Judith chimed in. 'It's in your eyes every time you say his name.'

'And he's right for you.' Holly paused. 'You're not still pretending to him that you've got a boyfriend, are you?'

'No.' Hardly, after what they'd done together.

'So what's the problem?' Holly asked.

Where did she start?

'Zo, you normally know exactly what you want and go for it,' Holly said. 'You're the most focused and organised person I know.'

'What's so different here?' Judith added.

'I…just… Look, I…' Zoe growled in frustration. How could she explain it, without telling her two best friends in the world that she hadn't trusted them with her darkest secret? And she'd left it too long to spill the beans now. She didn't want to hurt them. 'Enough of the grilling. It's not going to work and that's that.'

'How do you know unless you give it a try? What have you got to lose?' Holly asked, squeezing her hand.

Everything, Zoe thought, but didn't say it. She forced a smile to her face and switched the subject. 'There's ice-cream in the restaurant kitchen. It's got my name on it and it's calling to me.'

'OK, OK. We'll let you have your ice-cream,' Judith said. 'But promise me you'll think about it. He's perfect.'

Yeah. But I'm not, Zoe howled inwardly. *I'm not.* And I don't think I could bear his pity.

Three days later, Brad sat in his office, clicking his pen on and off. Zoe was driving him completely mad. He couldn't fault her at work—her patient care was meticulous, she spent time reassuring the parents and explaining to them what treatment she was giving and why, and he'd found her coaching one of the house officers through some tricky procedures. As a doctor and a colleague, she was top-notch.

As a woman…she was driving him crazy. He loved her. And, from her reactions to him at the cottage, he had an idea that she felt the same way about him. Zoe wasn't the sort to hop into bed with anyone who asked. She was choosy. So the fact that she'd made love with him *meant* something.

The fact that she'd virtually dumped him the next morning… That wasn't like her. Not the warm, generous, giving woman he'd come to know. Which meant that someone in her past had clearly hurt her so much that she didn't trust men. Brad figured that she'd called a halt precisely to make sure that *she* was the one saying it had to stop, not him—dump before being dumped. So he had to prove to her that she could trust him, that he wasn't just out for a quick lay. That she really could rely on him.

The question was, how?

He went back to clicking his pen. Maybe if he sat here long enough, he'd come up with a brilliant idea. Or maybe not.

The following day, Zoe knocked on Brad's door. 'Can I borrow your office for a while, please?' she asked.

'Sure. Problem?'

'Parents who need a bit of space,' she said. 'I have to tell them that their son's got haemophilia.'

'A or B?'

'A,' she said.

'Good. Telling parents that their child has Christmas disease—' the other name for haemophilia B, named after

the surname of the child who'd first had the condition
'—at this time of year could be a bit…' He pulled a face.

'Exactly.'

'Want some back-up?'

For a long, long moment, he thought she was going to
refuse. And then she nodded. 'Please.'

She was going to trust him. At work, admittedly, but it
was a start. If she trusted him at London City General,
she might come to realise she could trust him in her personal life, too. He smiled at her. 'I'll organise some coffee. How old's the little boy?'

'Toddler.'

'I'll sort some juice for him.'

A few minutes later, Zoe had introduced him to Colin
and Nadine Saunders and their eighteen-month-old son,
Harry.

'It's serious, isn't it?' Colin asked.

'Yes, but he's not going to die,' Zoe reassured him.
'And, Nadine, you can stop worrying that people think
you're hitting Harry. The bruising is nothing to do with
you. It's caused by moderate haemophilia.'

'Haemophilia?' Nadine's face whitened. 'Oh, my God.
Isn't that where you just bleed to death?'

'No—a lot of people think a haemophiliac can bleed to
death if he pricks his finger, but that isn't true. It's a blood
condition where an essential clotting factor is partly or
completely missing,' Brad explained. 'That causes someone who has haemophilia to bleed for longer than normal.
If Harry cuts or grazes himself, you should be able to stop
the bleeding with a little pressure and a plaster. The main
worry is if he bleeds internally into his joints, muscles or
soft tissues, so if he has a fall you need to bring him in
so we can check him over.'

'It's an inherited condition through the X chromosome,'

Zoe said. 'That's why it affects men rather than women—a man has only one X chromosome, so if it carries the haemophilia gene, he'll have haemophilia. A woman has two X chromosomes, so if one of her chromosomes has the haemophilia gene, she'll be a carrier and there's a fifty per cent chance that her son will have haemophilia and her daughter will be a carrier.'

'So it's my fault,' Nadine whispered. 'I gave it to him. But…there isn't anyone with haemophilia in my family.'

'In a third of all cases of haemophilia, there's no family history of the condition,' Brad said. 'It's a spontaneous genetic change and nobody knows why it happens.'

'Queen Victoria's probably the most famous case where that happened,' Zoe said.

'No blue blood on either side of our family, is there, love?' Colin said, clearly trying to lighten the atmosphere. 'So what does it mean for Harry, having haemophilia?'

'He's got haemophilia A—that means his factor VIII is lower than it should be, though in severe cases it's missing completely. At the moment Harry's condition is moderate, and often we don't pick up moderate cases of haemophilia until toddlerhood, when the child's always falling over and knocking itself,' Zoe said. 'Sometimes a fall will dislodge a clot and he'll start bleeding again.'

'He always bruises so badly. I'm sure our doctor thought I was hitting him, because he shouldn't have had bruises that big from just tripping over or knocking himself on a chair,' Nadine said.

Zoe smiled reassuringly. 'She didn't think that at all. She thought Harry might be a haemophiliac—that's why she sent you to us to ask for a blood test to check how Harry's blood is clotting. The test showed that his activated partial thromboplastin time or APTT—that's how we measure clotting—is longer than it should be.'

'So are we going to have to wrap him in cotton wool for the rest of his life?' Colin asked.

'No—he should be able to lead a more or less normal life, though I wouldn't advise that he takes up any contact sports such as rugby,' Brad said. 'Twenty years or so ago, Harry would have had a greatly reduced life expectancy, he'd have been crippled with arthritis and joint deformity by his teens and he'd have had to go to a special school for disabled children. Now he can go to a normal school, his life expectancy will be pretty much average, and he can get married, have children and do almost any job.'

'Children?' Nadine asked. 'But won't his children have it, too?'

'Not necessarily. There's a fifty per cent chance that his daughters will be carriers, but his sons won't be affected,' Zoe said.

'Does he have to take anything?' Colin asked.

Brad nodded. 'We'll replace the factor VIII in his blood with something called a coagulation factor concentrate. His body can't absorb factor VIII from his gastrointestinal tract, so we can't give it in tablet form. He'll need regular injections two or three times a week, and that should help to prevent any joint bleeds.'

'How will we know if he's got a joint bleed?' Nadine asked.

'It's most likely to be his knees, elbows, ankles, shoulders or wrists. There'll be some swelling, though this might only be slight, and he might say he feels a warm, prickly feeling and then it hurts.' Zoe sighed. 'The main problem is that once he's had a bleed into a joint, he's likely to bleed in that joint again, and it'll become more and more stiff. The more the joint swells, the more the cartilage and bone will degenerate.'

'So if he has a fall, bring him here?' Nadine asked.

'Yes, though we'll also be able to teach you how to give him the coagulation factor injections at home. When he's old enough, he'll be able to do it for himself.'

'A bit like a diabetic?' Colin asked.

'Pretty much,' Zoe said with a smile.

'You'll need to make sure they know about his condition at toddler group, nursery and school as he grows older—any doubts, get him here,' Brad said.

'We can put you in touch with a support group, so you can talk to other parents who've been through what you're going through right now,' Zoe told them.

'Thank you,' Nadine said. She looked at the little boy, who was busily taking bricks out of the box in the corner of Brad's office. 'If it wasn't for the bruising, I wouldn't think there's anything wrong with him.'

'He'll be able to lead a normal life,' Brad repeated. 'If he needs any dental treatment, they may be able to use fibrin glue. It's made of something called human thrombin and human fibrinogen. The dentist will spray them separately onto any wound, and they'll form a thin film of fibrin, which will help stop any bleeding, and Harry's body will gradually reabsorb the fibrin. It won't hurt or cause him any problems.'

'Couldn't you use the glue to stop any bleeding into the joints?' Colin asked.

'No—it'd cause a fatal blood clot. It's something you can use on the skin but not inside the body,' Brad explained.

When the Saunders family had left, Zoe turned to Brad. 'Thanks for your help.'

'No problem. We're a good team, Dr Kennedy,' he said lightly.

'Yeah.' She looked solemn. 'Brad, I...' She sighed.

He waited for her to finish, knowing now was the

wrong time to push. She needed to tell him whatever it was of her own accord, not be bulldozed into it. But then she turned away. 'I'd better go and write up my notes. Catch you later.'

'Sure.'

For the next week, Zoe kept up the polite-but-distant act, always having a good excuse why she couldn't have lunch or even a coffee-break with him. She seemed to vanish at the end of her shift before he could ask her if she'd like to go out for a meal, to the cinema, to the theatre—anything, as long as she spent time with him.

And every frustrating day of that week, he didn't get a chance to talk to her about anything except work. She didn't even ask him to help out at the Wednesday night fund-raiser the following week. It stung, but he guessed she was trying to keep him at arm's length. Fair enough, but it closed another avenue to him: it meant he couldn't ask Holly and Judith to help. Enlisting the aid of her best friends would put yet another wall between them, not to mention the damage it would do to her friendship with Holly and Judith.

The only bright spot was one time when she was walking along, reading a report at the same time, and collided with him. For a few brief moments he had a good excuse to keep her in his arms, because he was stopping her from falling. He felt her heart rate speed up as he held her, and smiled wryly to himself. She might be telling him to back off, but her body wasn't transmitting the same message. Zoe Kennedy wasn't as immune to him as she liked to make out. But how was he going to get her to give him a chance?

And then it hit him. They were both off on the Friday after the monthly fund-raiser. If he could talk her into spending the day with him—ostensibly to show him the sights of London, as a friend—he'd change the plan at the last minute. Suggest a picnic somewhere. And if they were using his transport rather than her car... Yes. He grinned. Perfect. He'd hire a Harley. She'd have to trust his driving to keep them both safe—and, being a pillion passenger, she'd have to hold him. If that didn't melt her, nothing would.

On the Wednesday night, Brad swapped shifts so he could go to the fund-raiser. Zoe, as usual, was busy at the back, and because it was the Christmas fund-raiser, it was busy and Brad couldn't push through the crowds to reach her. Everywhere he looked there were Santa hats covered with glitter and sequins and the occasional flashing stars. Judith was in fine form, with a set full of Christmas songs to get people in the mood.

And then Holly spotted him. 'Hi! Come to do a guest spot for us?' she asked.

'Um, I...'

'Go on. Sing something for our Zo.'

Brad looked at her suspiciously. Did she know something? Had Zoe talked to her about him? But Holly looked completely innocent.

She pushed him onto the stage and Judith winked at him. 'Excellent! Now we can do all the Christmas duets.'

He sat at the piano and Judith moved her stool to sit next to him. 'White Christmas', 'Rocking around the Christmas tree' and 'Baby, it's cold outside' followed in swift succession. And then Judith mouthed at him, 'Sing something for Zo.'

It was too much of a coincidence, both her best friends asking him to sing something for her. This had to be a coded message from them to woo her, in the way that only he could. He smiled, and played the first chords of 'She's the one'.

Zoe, at the back of the hall, went rigid. Please, don't let this be Brad singing on his own, she begged silently. Don't let him be singing this for me.

But when he started singing and Jude didn't join in, Zoe realised that he'd picked this song for a purpose. For her. Telling her that he wanted her.

And how she wanted him. But he was singing to a woman who didn't exist. Zoe Kennedy, whole of heart and whole of body. The real Zoe Kennedy was someone else. And her heart was splintering with every single word he sang.

She couldn't face him. Or Judith, or Holly. So she slipped quietly over to the bar. 'Fin, can I have a word?'

'Sure, Zoe,' the bar manager said. 'What's up?'

'I've got a splitting headache.' It wasn't a complete untruth. Her head did ache. But her heart ached more. 'I'm probably going down with something. You know what it's like, this time of year.'

'Especially on your ward. Kids pick up everything going and pass it on to the doctors and nurses,' Fin said wryly.

'So I'm calling it a night. I think I need some sleep. Could you get someone to help with the clearing up, please?'

'Course I can.'

'Thanks, Fin. I owe you one,' Zoe said feelingly. 'I'll pay for any extra overtime.'

'Don't worry about that—I'll do it myself. Just save me some of your brownies next time you make a batch.'

'I'll do some especially for you,' Zoe promised. 'When Jude finishes her set, can you tell her or Holls that I've gone home and I'm unplugging the phone so I can get some sleep?'

'Sure. Take care, sweetheart,' Fin said.

At least now I've got a breathing space, Zoe thought as she slipped quietly out of the hospital social club. Until tomorrow. When one or all three of them will expect an explanation. And by then I'll have a decent cover story.

Except she didn't. She slept badly, thinking of Brad and wishing for what she couldn't have. The next morning, her head felt stuffed with cotton wool and even a tepid shower didn't do much to make her feel awake.

'Got a minute?' Brad asked, virtually as soon as Zoe walked onto the ward.

'Uh, sure.' She gave him her very best smile.

'My office,' he said quietly.

As if it were a professional matter. But she had a nasty feeling this wasn't about work. This was about last night. She sighed inwardly. Better to get it over with. She followed him to his office and he closed the door behind her.

'Take a seat.'

She did so.

'How's your head?'

'All right,' she mumbled.

'You look better than I expected. Fin told us you were going down with the lurgy.'

How to get caught out telling lies, she thought wryly. 'I thought I was.'

'Zoe. We're friends, right?'

That wasn't quite what she'd expected him to say. She looked at him, and realised her mistake. Because those blue, blue eyes told her that he knew everything.

Well, almost everything. There was one thing he couldn't possibly know.

'Friends,' she agreed.

'And you're off duty tomorrow.'

'Ye-es.' Where was this leading?

'So am I. I'm going to play tourist. Come with me?'

She couldn't. She had something to do. A pressing appointment. Errands. Anything. Tell him no, her mind said urgently. 'Yes,' her mouth said.

'Good. I'll pick you up tomorrow at ten.'

'You want to see the sights by car? Brad, parking in central London's a nightmare. Not to mention the congestion charge and the fact you won't get to see anything because you'll be herded around by the taxis. You'll see a lot more if we take the Tube and walk.'

He spread his hands. 'OK. I'll meet you tomorrow at ten, at your place.'

'Where are we going?'

'Depends on the weather. I thought we could go and feed the pigeons in Trafalgar Square or something.'

'No, I'm afraid the pigeons have all but disappeared.' She blinked hard. 'And, anyway, you've obviously never seen *The Birds*.'

'The Hitchcock film?'

She nodded. 'That's what it was like, believe me.'

'What do you suggest, then?'

'It's too cold for a boat ride down to Kew. But we could do the Aquarium.'

'And feed the sharks… Great idea.' He winked. 'See you later.'

'That was it? That's what you wanted to talk to me about?'

'Zo, we're so busy on the ward we don't get time to breathe, let alone speak to each other.'

And his face said he knew quite well she'd been avoiding him on a personal level ever since their weekend at the seaside.

Maybe this was his way of showing her that they could be friends. And if they were doing touristy things, it couldn't get too personal between them—could it?

CHAPTER ELEVEN

THE next morning was bright and cold. Absolutely perfect, Brad thought. Forget the picnic. They'd go for a drive in the country, stop for a pub lunch, then maybe go for a walk by a river or something—and this time they'd walk hand in hand. He put the spare helmet into the top box of the Harley, made sure his own was secure and rode over to Zoe's house. He parked the bike as near to her terrace as possible, then rang her doorbell.

'Hi.' She opened the door and smiled at him. 'Ready for the sharks?'

'No. There's a slight change of plan,' he said as she locked her front door.

She frowned. 'How do you mean?'

'It's a beautiful day.' He was still holding the motorcycle helmet behind his back, keeping the surprise as long as he could. 'I thought we could go into the country. Have a pub lunch, then a long walk—that sort of thing.'

'Sure. We could try Epping Forest. It's really pretty around there.' She rummaged in her bag. 'My car keys are in here somewhere.'

'No need. I'm driving.'

She rolled her eyes. 'Don't tell me—you've found yourself a sports car. Let me guess—bright red or British racing green?'

'Neither.' He shepherded her over to the Harley and gave her a brief bow. 'Our transport, *mademoiselle*.'

She gazed at it in seeming disbelief, then at him, her

eyes wide and filled with shock and hurt and growing fury. Her lip curled. 'You stupid, stupid bastard!'

Brad stared at her. He'd never, ever heard Zoe swear, not even mildly. But he'd also never seen her look this angry. 'Zo? What's the problem? It's perfectly safe. I've got a spare motorcycle helmet for you in the top box. And the pillion's comfortable. That's why I hired it.'

'You must be bloody joking! No *way* am I going on that thing!'

She was shaking, and her face was so white that for a moment Brad thought she was going to be sick.

'Zo? What's wrong?'

She shook her head, her mouth working as if she was trying to explain but the words just weren't coming out. Then she turned and ran into the house. Her front door crashed hard behind her.

Brad was too stunned to move. All he'd done had been to suggest she ride pillion with him, and Zoe had gone bananas. She'd overreacted big time.

But Zoe wasn't a drama queen. This really wasn't like her. Clearly motorbikes hit a raw nerve for her. Maybe a past boyfriend had died on a motorbike—or even a brother, because she hadn't spoken much about her family except for her aunt Jay and her scatterbrained cousin Ned.

Hell. He'd had no idea she'd react so badly. But he certainly wasn't going to leave things like this. He rang her doorbell, but she refused to answer. He rang again. Still no answer. Even when he leaned on the doorbell, she ignored him.

He changed tactics, and counted in his head as he rang the doorbell again. One-two. Pause. One-two. Pause. He doubled the pace. One, two, three, four. Doubled it again: no way would she be able to hold out against this, and he was prepared to stand there all day jabbing the doorbell until she answered. One-and-two-and-three-and-four-and—

The door was yanked open. 'Go away,' Zoe said through gritted teeth.

'I'm not going anywhere, Zoe. Not until you've talked to me.'

'I don't want to talk.'

'You might not want to,' he said softly, 'but you *need* to. Let me in. Please.'

He thought she was going to slam the door in his face, but eventually she sighed and stood aside.

'So are you going to tell me what that was all about?' he asked as he closed the front door behind him.

'What?'

'The bike.'

'There's nothing to tell,' she muttered.

Nothing? He didn't believe that for a second. 'What was it you once said to me? It's better out than in. And you were absolutely right. So isn't it time you talked, too? Tell me,' he said softly. 'What happened to make you hate motorbikes so much?'

'I don't want to talk about it.'

She was white and shaking again. Brad dropped the motorcycle helmet and took her hands. 'Zo, this is me. Friends, remember? Whatever you tell me stays with me, and me only. I'm not going to spread it round the hospital grapevine.'

'There's nothing to tell,' she said again.

'Yes, there is,' he insisted, as gently as he could. 'Talk to me, Zo. What happened? Was it your brother?'

'I'm an only child.'

'Then what?'

Her hands balled into fists and she pulled away from

his grasp. 'You really want to know?' Her eyes challenged him.

He nodded.

'All right, then. *This* is what happened.' She yanked her sweater off and chucked it on the floor; her bra followed suit. She stood with her chin lifted and her teeth clenched, her face daring him to make a comment. Her left breast was covered with scars, as was her left arm from just above the elbow to her shoulder.

He sucked in his breath. 'Oh, Zoe.'

'So now you know, you can just go away again, can't you?' Her voice was thick with unshed tears.

'Actually, no. I can't. This happened on a bike?'

She nodded.

'My poor Zoe.'

'Don't you *dare* pity me,' she said through gritted teeth.

'I'm not. Believe me, Zoe, pity's the last thing I feel for you.' He knew exactly where she was coming from. He'd been there and he knew how bad it felt. 'You once told me that you weren't offering me pity. I'm not offering it to you either.' He picked her sweater up and gave it back to her. 'Put your sweater on.'

Her eyes glimmered with tears. 'Because how I look…it's disgusting.'

'No, honey. It's because you haven't got any net curtains in your living room.'

'What?' Her brow furrowed.

'Unless you want to flash the street, you need to put your sweater on. Or leave it off and I'll draw the curtains. Either way's fine by me.'

She stared at him in blank incomprehension. 'What are you talking about?'

'We're going into your living room. You're going to

sit down and tell me all about it. On your sofa. Face to face.'

'I...'

She was shaking again, and a single tear spilled down her cheek. Brad wiped it away with his thumb, stroked her face, then took the sweater from her and gently helped her into it. Then he picked her up and carried her into the living room.

'Put me down,' she said through gritted teeth.

'Sure.' He sat down on the sofa and kept his arms tightly round her so she was forced to sit on his lap.

'Brad—'

'Don't even think about asking me to let you go, Zoe Kennedy. I'm not going to. You're staying right here, with me, and I'm not going anywhere.' He kissed the tip of her nose. 'Tell me what happened. All of it. Right from the beginning. I'm not going to judge, I'm just going to listen.'

She was silent for a long, long time. He saw her swallow hard. And then she spoke, her voice an agonised whisper.

'I met Dermot at college. He was the year above me. He was an art student, a bit of a bad boy. I suppose he was my teenage rebellion—my parents were horrified that my first serious boyfriend had long hair and an earring. And a motorbike.' She took a deep, shuddering breath. 'He bought me my own helmet and I used to ride pillion. We went everywhere together on the bike. But Dermot never took risks—not when I was with him at least. I suppose I thought I could redeem my bad boy. And he was gorgeous. He could have had his pick of girls in the sixth form. I never thought he'd look twice at me—little and plump and plain.'

Pocket-sized Venus, and completely unaware of how

lovely she was, more like, Brad thought. Zoe wasn't the type to fish for compliments.

'But he did. The college swot and the college rebel, an item. Nobody ever thought it would last. But it worked. It just worked. I could be myself with Dermot. I wasn't just plain, plump, swotty Zoe Kennedy. He made me beautiful, Brad. I felt like a princess when I was with him. Out of all the girls who fell at his feet, he'd chosen me. And we had plans—he was going to art college, I was going to med school, and when we'd both qualified we were going to travel, do a couple of years' foreign aid work. Maybe settle down abroad and raise a family.

'Then, one day, we were out on the bike and this car was coming too fast towards us round a bend—it was on our side of the road. Dermot had to swerve to stop it crashing into us. The bike hit a stone and we both came off. Dermot went head-on into the car. I was lucky, I just hit the road. I landed on my left side. The, um, leather jacket wasn't quite enough protection. I broke a couple of ribs and needed some skin grafts.'

Typical Zoe to understate it. They'd been painful grafts, from the look of her arm and her breast.

'And Dermot?' Brad asked quietly.

Zoe closed her eyes. 'He died. The paramedics said he broke his neck and died almost instantly. There was nothing anyone could have done to save him.'

So she'd lost someone she loved, too. 'That's why you understood about Lara.'

'Yeah. Though I didn't get the pity or the sympathy from people after his death.' She opened her eyes again and her face tightened. 'I got everyone telling me it was probably for the best, that Dermot was no good for me and all the rest of it, and at least now I wasn't going to be stupid and drop out of college halfway through my A-levels.'

'You were only seventeen when it happened?'

'Sixteen,' she corrected. 'I was taking my exams a year early.'

He wasn't surprised. From what he'd seen of Zoe on the ward, he already knew she was bright.

'My parents were convinced that Dermot and I were having underage sex—especially with Dermot's reputation at college. Though we actually waited until I was sixteen.' A sad, fleeting smile crossed her lips. 'My sixteenth birthday. We went to Brighton. He'd saved his money from his Saturday job and booked us a hotel room. The honeymoon suite, overlooking the sea. And…' Her voice faded as if the memories were too precious to speak of.

'You really loved him.' It was a statement, not a question.

She nodded. 'The only ones who understood were his parents. And Jay. She fetched me from Kent and made me stay with her until I'd healed. I took a year out of school.'

'And that's when you went beachcombing?'

'Yes. I thought about dropping out of school completely. Then Jay pointed out that if I did, I'd be cutting off my nose to spite my face, because I really wanted to be a doctor. And if I didn't go to med school, I'd be letting myself down and everyone would blame Dermot. Which wasn't fair, because Dermot had always encouraged me. He actually used to make me study. He used to sketch me while I was working. All that bad boy stuff…he wasn't that much of a rebel really. But everyone judged him on the way he looked, the earring and the hair and the jacket and the bike. And the fact that he walked out of his classes—but his history of art teacher was truly useless and spent the lessons babbling about television and trying to be mates with the students. Dermot borrowed the A-level syllabus, copied it in longhand and was working through it on his own in the library. He'd have got top grades in everything.' Her voice cracked. 'But he died three months before he could take his exams. It was such a waste. Such a bloody *waste*.'

Brad knew exactly what she meant. He'd howled the same thing himself the day that Lara had died.

'I mourned Dermot. I missed him. But I went back to school, took my exams and university was a new start for me. I met Holls and Jude and we had a great time—I used to cook for us, they'd do the washing-up and then we'd go to the pictures or just sit listening to records and drinking red wine and chatting. The usual student stuff. And then I met…' She screwed her face up. 'Hell, I can't even remember his name now. Tim? Todd? Anyway, he wasn't a medic. He was a history student. He made me laugh. I really thought it was going to work. He wasn't the love of my life or anything like that, but I thought we'd have fun together and I'd learn to enjoy life again.

'Then one night, after a party, we went back to his room. We'd had a bit too much to drink and we started kissing, touching.' She sighed. 'It was my own fault. I hadn't told him about my scars and it must have been a real shock for him. He, um, didn't react very well when he discovered them.'

Brad said nothing, just stroked her hair and urged her silently to talk.

'He said I was—' her voice dropped to a hoarse whisper '—damaged goods.'

'He said *what*?' Brad balled his fists.

'Damaged goods,' Zoe repeated.

Brad shook his head. 'No way. Absolutely no way,' he said through gritted teeth, wanting to flatten Tim or Todd or whatever his name was. He held her closer. 'They're skin deep, Zoe. Surface.'

'Yeah. But he had a point. They look…' She shook her head.

'So that's why you didn't want me to take your pyjama top off—in case I reacted the same way as your boyfriend?'

'Yes—no—I don't know. I didn't think you'd reject me, exactly. But…I just couldn't tell you.'

It wasn't personal, Brad knew that. It was because of the boyfriend who'd crushed her confidence all those years before and left her too scared to trust.

'I thought you'd pity me. Feel obliged to stay with me because I'm…damaged. Not because you wanted to be with me.'

'Well, you thought wrong. I don't pity you and I don't feel under any obligation. I'm here precisely because I *want* to be here.' He dropped a kiss on her temple. 'Because I want to be with *you,* Zoe Kennedy. With the woman who brightens my day just by walking into the same room as me.'

She said nothing, but he felt her take a deep, shuddering breath.

'Do Holly and Judith know about him?' he asked quietly.

'Dermot?'

'The other one.'

She shook her head. 'I never told them.'

Something in her voice alerted him. 'What about Dermot and the accident? Do they know about that?'

She closed her eyes. 'No. And I've never been swimming with them and I don't sunbathe, so they've never had an opportunity to see the scars.'

'They're your best friends, Zo. Why didn't you tell them?'

She flinched. 'It's not the kind of thing you bring up when you're getting to know people. And when Tim— Todd, whatever his name was—said it, it just hurt too much to talk about it. And then I'd kept it quiet for so long, it would have felt wrong to tell them—as if I hadn't trusted them enough. As if I'd held back on our friendship. Which I suppose I have.' Her mouth tightened. 'I'm a fake.'

'No, you're not. And you're not damaged goods, Zoe. You're beautiful.'

She swallowed. 'Brad, you're a nice man. A good man. You deserve someone who—'

'You,' he cut in swiftly.

'But—'

'No buts. I want you, Zoe. That's what today was about. I guessed that someone had hurt you, made you lose your trust in men. So I thought if I got you on the back of a bike, you'd have to trust me to keep you safe, and then once you trusted me you'd let me close to you. Oh, and you'd have to hold me while I was driving. So I'd planned to take the longest possible route. Though I promise you, if I'd had the remotest idea about what happened to you, I wouldn't have sprung it on you.' He paused. 'I take it you haven't been within a mile of a bike since the accident.'

She smiled wryly. 'What do you think?'

Judging by her reaction a few minutes ago, no. 'But you enjoyed riding with Dermot?'

'Yes.'

'Then maybe it's time you got back on a motorbike. It

would get your confidence back and help you remember the good times with Dermot.'

She shook her head. 'Thanks for the offer but no. I don't want to go on a motorbike ever, ever again. And I don't want your pity.'

He smiled. 'You're not listening to me, are you? Pity's the last thing I feel where you're concerned.'

'Is it?'

'Look into my eyes. Tell me what you see,' he urged softly.

'I...'

'Do you see pity?'

'No.'

'What do you see, Zoe?'

She was silent. Almost as if she was afraid to say it, afraid that by voicing it aloud she'd break the spell.

'I'll tell you, shall I?' he whispered. 'Desire. Lust. You have no idea how many cold showers I've needed since that night we shared. Or the kind of dreams that wake me. Or how many times I've had to stop myself dragging you into a linen cupboard at the hospital and having my wicked way with you.'

Her cheeks became tinged with pink. 'Really?'

'Really.' He took her hand and placed it over his heart. 'If I just felt sorry for you, would my heart be beating this hard, this fast?'

'I don't know,' she mumbled.

He lifted her hand to his face, dropped a kiss in her palm and curled his fingers over it. 'It wouldn't, Zo, and you know it. You do things to me. You have, almost since the first day I met you. There was something about you— the way you were determined to make me a part of the hospital, not an interloper on secondment. You wouldn't take no for an answer.' He smiled. 'Hurricane Zoe. But it was more than that. I'd kept my emotions in cold storage, and you thawed me. And when we were at the cottage, I discovered something.' He stroked her face. 'Something I wasn't expecting. I didn't think I'd ever love again after Lara died—but you've changed all that.'

'Me?'

He nodded. 'You. I love you, Zoe. And I want to be with you. If you'll have me.'

'I…'

He saw the doubt in her eyes and pressed a finger to her lips. 'Shh. Don't talk. Don't think. Just feel. Remember when we fed each other ice-cream on this sofa? And I kissed you.' He bent his head and touched his lips to hers. Softly, gently, coaxing her. 'And you kissed me back,' he murmured.

To his delight, she did.

'But this time I want more. Much, much more. So either we close the curtains or you'd better hope that nobody's going to look through your living-room window because I want to make love with you. Right here, right now. Skin to skin. I want to touch you, taste you—all over.'

'There's a third option.' Her voice sounded rusty. She stood up. Held out her hand, almost shyly.

Brad smiled, took her hand, and let her lead the way upstairs.

CHAPTER TWELVE

ZOE closed her bedroom curtains and Brad switched the bedside lamp on.

Her eyes widened. 'We can't...'

'Yes, we can. And, yes, we will,' he said softly. He took her hand and kissed each finger in turn. 'I want to see you, Zoe. All of you. Your scars are just another part of you. Believe me, they don't make any difference to the way I feel about you.'

Damaged goods. Damaged goods. The words echoed in her head.

It must have shown on her face, because Brad kissed the tip of her nose. 'Forget what he said. It's not true. Yes, you're scarred—but nobody's completely flawless. And, anyway, I don't want flawless. I want you.' He slid his hands under the edge of her sweater. 'Right now, I want to touch you. I want to make you feel as good as you make me feel.'

A shiver ran down her spine as his fingertips splayed over her abdomen. Last time he'd touched her like this, it had been in his sleep. She'd left before he could discover her secret. This time... This time, he already knew about it.

She let him remove her sweater and drop it on the floor. And then she tensed. He'd said it didn't matter. But if she looked, she knew she'd see pity in his eyes. Pity and revulsion and—

'Look at me, Zoe,' he commanded softly, as if he'd read her thoughts.

It was hard. Very hard. But finally she raised her gaze to meet his. And what she saw took her breath away. His pupils were huge with desire and the cornflower-blue irises were tiny rings around them. No pity. No revulsion. Just wonder, a wonder that had to be reflected on her own face.

'Keep looking at me,' he said, and raised her left hand to his mouth. He kissed the pads of her fingers in turn, his lips nibbling teasingly at her skin. Ran his tongue along the V between her thumb and index finger. Kissed her palm then made a trail of tiny kisses to her wrist. Her pulse was beating madly and his tongue pressed against it, promising more. He kissed his way up to the sensitive spot in the crook of her elbow.

And then he shuddered, a second before he reached her scarred upper arm.

Zoe pulled away as if he'd scalded her. 'No.'

'Did that hurt?'

Yes, but not in the way he meant.

'Zo, I'm sorry. It didn't even occur to me that your skin might be sensitive there.'

'It isn't,' she muttered.

He drew her into his arms, stroked her hair. 'Then what's wrong? Am I taking this too fast for you?'

'No. But you're only doing this to be kind.'

'No, I'm not.'

She pulled back and stared at him in shock. 'What?'

'I'm not being kind.'

'I said that aloud?' She forced the words through dry lips.

'Mmm-hmm. Though even if you hadn't, it was written all over your face. And I can assure you, I'm not doing this out of duty or kindness or pity. That wasn't revulsion you felt. That was me on the edge of losing my self-

control because I want you so much.' Colour slashed
across his cheekbones. 'Whatever you might have heard
about medical students or lifeguards, I was never one for
sleeping around. I've always been choosy. I was always
faithful to Lara. And you were the first woman I'd even
kissed since she died, let alone spent the night with.'

'Oh.' Zoe bit her lip. She'd done him an injustice. 'I'm
sorry.'

'So am I,' he said quietly. 'Sorry that you've had years
of feeling you're a failure instead of realising that you're
a beautiful woman.'

'You're overdoing it,' she said with a rueful smile. 'I'm
just ordinary.'

'I disagree. Want to know what I see?'

She wasn't sure that she did.

'I see a heart-shaped face.' He traced the shape of her
jaw with his thumb. 'Beautiful deep brown eyes that I
could never say no to. A mouth that makes me ache with
wanting.' He rubbed his thumb against her lower lip, then
let his hand drop lower; his index finger traced her ster-
num. 'A cleavage that any man would fight sharks to dive
into.'

She giggled. 'Oh, for goodness' sake!'

He grinned. 'That's better. Seriously, Zo, you're gorgeous. You just keep your lovely, lush curves hidden beneath baggy sweaters.' He smiled at her. 'And, as consultant on your ward, I'm pulling rank. So you're
officially beautiful, Zoe Kennedy. Got it?'

She nodded. 'Got it.'

'Good.' He kissed the inside of her wrist. 'Before I
carry on—does it hurt? Physically, I mean, when I touch
your skin?' He brushed his lips lightly over the skin at
the very edge of her scars.

She shook her head. 'That's…' Nobody had ever kissed her there. 'That's fine,' she said shakily.

His smile broadened. 'Excellent. Now, where were we?' Brad licked the inside of her elbow. 'You smell good, Zo. You taste good. And I'm going to touch you. Taste you. All over. I'm going to kiss you better, Zoe. And then some.'

His lips travelled over the scar tissue on her arm. Zoe felt the tears welling up and tried to blink them back, but one escaped and splashed against his skin. Brad straightened up and cupped her face in his hands. 'Don't cry, honey. I promise, it's going to be all right. I love you, remember? And that's all of you, Zoe, from the top of your head to the ends of your toes—and everything in between.'

She was too choked to reply.

'I love you,' he repeated. 'And that's for keeps.'

For keeps. She sucked in a breath. This couldn't be happening. They'd first met barely a couple of months before.

But she'd known the instant she'd met him that he was special. And when they'd made love, she'd known that she loved him. 'I love you, too,' she said, her voice hesitant and whispery.

She got her reward instantly, because Brad picked her up, carried her over to the queen-sized bed, nudged her duvet to one side and laid her down gently on the sheet. He sprawled beside her and undid the top button of her jeans. 'That's settled, then,' he said, his voice husky. 'You love me and I love you. And now we're going to make some memories to wipe out the past. Not Dermot, not Lara—we'll both always remember them, always have a corner of our hearts reserved for them, and that's the way it should be—but whatever his name was. The stupid kid who couldn't see past the end of his nose. His loss, and most definitely my gain.'

He circled her navel with a teasing finger, then let his finger drift a little lower to stroke the warm, soft skin of her abdomen. As it slid under the edge of her knickers, Zoe shivered and lifted her hips slightly.

'Impatient, are we?' he murmured.

Zoe blushed, and he chuckled. 'I was planning to take my time. Explore a little. But since you have other ideas…' He undid her zip. Lifted her slightly. Slid the faded denims down her body.

'Mmm. This is good.' He almost purred with satisfaction as he touched her.

'No, it isn't. You're fully clothed,' she pointed out.

'Mmm. And I want to be skin to skin with you. Going to help me?'

There was a wickedly sexy tilt to his mouth, and she couldn't resist. She sat up, slid her arms around his neck and kissed him. It didn't matter any more that the light was on. That he could see her scars, feel the bumpiness of her skin. She wasn't sure which of them removed the rest of his clothing—and hers—but the next thing she knew, Brad was kneeling next to her. His head dipped and he traced the line of her collarbone with his tongue. One hand cupped her right breast, stroking it gently and teasing the peak until she was arching her back. And then she felt his mouth over her left breast. His lips travelled the length of her scars, kissing away the nightmares. And then his mouth opened over her nipple, sucking and licking until she was gasping.

'My beautiful Zoe,' he murmured against her skin, and then he kissed his way down her body. His mouth teased her, incited her until she was yelling and her climax crashed through her.

She called out his name, and he was there beside her, cradling her in his arms.

'I wanted the first time to be for you,' he whispered, rubbing his nose against hers. 'The first time we were properly skin to skin.'

The kissing began again, and heat rose between them until Brad lifted her to straddle him. Part of Zoe wanted to cover herself with her hands, to hide her scarred breast and her arm, but he shook his head.

'I love you, remember,' he mouthed. 'You don't have to hide anything from me.'

She nodded, and began to move over him. As she felt her climax begin to rise again and her breathing became shallow, Brad supported her, keeping her upright until she reached the peak. Pleasure surged through her and she tipped her head back. Brad sat up and held her closely to him, kissing her throat as he reached his own climax.

Afterwards, she lay curled in his arms, not bothering to pull the duvet over them. He was right. The scars *didn't* matter. Nothing mattered except lying here with him.

Her stomach rumbled, and Brad chuckled. 'Didn't you have breakfast?'

'Yes. But it was a long time ago.'

He glanced at the clock on her bedside. 'Mmm. Fair point. Though I suppose it's a bit too late to take you for that pub lunch.'

She stilled. 'I'm not going on a bike again, Brad.'

'I won't push you,' he reassured her.

'Good.'

'And you believe me now?'

'About what?'

'That these don't make any difference to me?' His fingertips lightly brushed her scars.

'I could do with a little more…persuasion,' she said.

He laughed, and rolled her onto her back. 'Later, I will. But there is something I want to talk to you about.'

Goose-bumps rose on her skin. 'What?'

'Don't look so worried.' He leaned over and kissed her. 'I'm a fairly traditional kind of guy.'

'Meaning?'

He slid off the bed, got down on one knee and held her hand. 'Will you marry me, Zoe?'

She blinked. Hard. 'Did you just ask me to marry you?'

'Mmm-hmm.'

'I…' She sat up. 'Brad, we haven't known each other very long.'

'Long enough for me to be sure.'

'What about Lara?'

He moved to sit beside her, still holding her hand. 'Like I said, I'll always love her. Just as you'll always love Dermot. But it's time for us both to move on.' His fingers tightened round hers. 'Lara would have liked you. She was very different from you, but I think you'd have been friends.'

'But, Brad—*marriage*. It's a big step. And don't you want a bride who can wear a princess dress with no shoulders and a huge net skirt? Someone a bit more…well, glamorous?'

'You don't need a princess dress to get married. The only thing I really want you to wear is a ring. My wedding ring.'

He hadn't said a thing about glamorous, she noted.

He sighed and put his arms round her. 'Oh, Zoe.' He kissed the tip of her nose. '*I* think you're beautiful. You're glamorous enough for me. But if you're that worried about your scars…plastic surgery has moved on a long way since you had the accident.'

She pulled back. 'Is that what you want? For me to

have more plastic surgery, to get rid of…all this?' She waved a hand at her scarred arm and breast.

'What I want,' he said quietly, 'is for you to be happy. If having surgery on your scars would make you happy, I'll support you all the way. If you don't want to have it done, that's also fine with me.'

Tears pricked her eyelids.

'It's your choice, Zo. Whatever you decide, I'll be there for you all the way.'

'I don't want surgery. Last time, the skin grafts…'

She didn't have to say any more. He held her close. 'I love you for yourself, Zo. Marry me.'

'I thought I was supposed to be the hurricane,' she said lightly.

He grinned. 'Hurricane Zoe, meet Tornado Brad.'

She grinned back. 'That's terrible. Seriously, don't you want someone who can breast-feed your babies?'

'I want you. And breast-feeding is your choice. If it doesn't work out, we'll bottle-feed. Which doesn't mean you're a failure—it means I'll be able to take my turn with the night shift and let you get some rest.' Then his pupils dilated, as if he'd just realised what she'd said.

Babies.

'You want to make babies with me?' He exhaled sharply. 'Zo…I want to make babies with you, too. But I'm… Hell.' He ran a hand through his hair. 'I'd better warn you now, I'm probably going to be over-protective throughout your pregnancy. Extremely over-protective. I'll want to go to every single antenatal with you and—'

'And one of my two best friends is an obstetrician,' she cut in. 'So I'm going to have plenty of people keeping an eye on me. What happened to Lara was tragic. But it's also extremely rare, and there's no reason why I should develop eclampsia or even pre-eclampsia.' She squeezed his hand. 'We'll deal with it together, when we have to. Heal each other's hurt.'

'So you'll marry me?'

'Small problem. When your grandchildren ask you how you proposed to me, how are you going to tell them it was while you were naked and in my bed?' She coughed. 'And you did say you were a traditional guy…'

'OK. Here's the deal. Late lunch—very late lunch,' he amended. 'A walk in the forest. And I'll propose to you there, in the middle of the trees with the birds singing all around us.'

She shook her head. 'Not today. It'll be dark by the time we get there—and Epping Forest is a spooky place at night. It's meant to be haunted by the spirit of Dick Turpin, the highwayman.'

'No forest, then.' He thought about it. 'If I find the perfect place for a proposal, are you going to say yes?'

She grinned. 'There's only one way for you to find out.'

'Ask you.' He spread his hands. 'OK. And I'll keep asking until you say yes.'

'Like that thing you did with my doorbell?'

He chuckled. 'It made you answer, didn't it? Hmm. I could learn Morse code and ask you via your doorbell.'

'Don't you dare!'

'What's it worth?' he teased.

'OK. I'll say yes. If you find the perfect place.'

'Not "if". It's "when".' He dropped a kiss on the end of her nose. 'I'll go make us some lunch.'

He borrowed a towel from her bathroom, slung it round his waist and headed for the kitchen. He returned a few minutes later with coffee and a huge plateful of cheese on toast.

'Domesticated. Mmm. That's just what I like to see,' she said, once she'd finished her lunch.

'I have a wild side, too. In fact, let me show you,' Brad said, and proceeded to demonstrate by making love to her so thoroughly that she was breathless.

Zoe made Brad breakfast the next morning, and they were both nearly late for work. When they reached the ward, they discovered that it had been decorated in their absence. Streamers hung on the walls, the first few cards drawn by patients were displayed on the doors and there was a huge Christmas tree in the reception area.

'We should have a Christmas wedding,' Brad muttered.

'You haven't asked me properly yet,' she muttered back. 'And there isn't enough time to arrange it.'

'Try me.'

'OK, a Christmas wedding—if it's *next* Christmas.'

Brad gasped. 'I can't wait that long!'

'You've got a ward round to do, Mr Hutton. And I've got a drug round.' She winked at him.

'Have lunch with me?'

'Sorry. I'm meeting Holls and Jude.'

'Going to tell them?'

'Maybe.'

'Tell them, or I'll gatecrash your lunch and tell them myself,' he threatened.

'Ha. Catch you later,' she said, and sauntered off to the drugs cabinet. Brad smiled and headed for the nurses' station, a spring in his step.

'Brad—just the person I wanted to see,' Erin said.

'Oh?'

'It's the ward bran tub,' she explained. 'We do it every year.'

'What is it?'

'Everyone who wants to be in it puts their name in the hat. You pick a name out, and you buy that person a present—anything you like, though there's a price limit. Some people buy something serious, some buy something really silly and fun.'

'Sure, I'm in,' he said. And then it hit him. This could be the perfect opportunity. 'When do you draw it?'

'Christmas Eve. For those who are on duty, that is— those who aren't take their present at the end of their last shift before then. Actually, we normally ask one of the consultants to do the draw.'

Better and better. 'I'm on duty Christmas Eve.' So was Zoe. 'I'll do the draw, if you like.'

'That's great. Thanks, Brad.'

'Who's in charge of the names?'

'Me.'

He slid an arm round her shoulders. 'Erin, honey, I'd like you to do me a teensy favour…'

'Sorry, sorry, sorry!' Holly sank into her chair. 'Uh. What a morning. Jude, we need you to come down and give us a tune in the Emergency Department. ''Here we end up with a Colles' fracture''—sung to the tune of ''Here we go round the mulberry bush''. Why is it that people have to walk outside on really frosty mornings?'

'To get to work,' Zoe said, chuckling.

'Not on a Saturday. They're off to play. But they don't wear sensible shoes, they fall over, they stick their hands out to stop them going flat on their faces and, bam! I reckon we've got the world record for Colles' fractures today,' Holly grumbled.

'Never mind, Holls. You've got twenty minutes' respite,' Judith said, pushing a plate across to her. 'I got you a turkey and cranberry baguette.'

'And I got us chocolate cake,' Zoe added.

Holly groaned in bliss. 'Thanks. Just what I need.

You're lifesavers. I haven't even had a chance to stop for a mouthful of water this morning.'

'Hint taken. I'll go and get us some coffee,' Zoe said.

'Mmm, it's my shout,' Holly mumbled through her baguette. She dug in her purse and handed Zoe a note.

When Zoe returned with three lattes, both Holly and Judith looked at her.

'What?' she asked.

'Something's happened,' Holly pronounced. 'You look different.'

'No, I don't.'

'Yes, you do,' Judith said. 'You look...radiant. Glowing. What have you done?'

'Nothing.'

'We're your best friends. You can't hide from us. What have you done?' Holly asked.

'Nothing. Yet.' Zoe tried to look solemn, though she couldn't stop a wide, wide smile. 'It's what I'm going to do. I need a bit of a favour from both of you.'

'Of course. What?' Judith asked.

'I need you to come dress shopping with me.'

Holly frowned. 'But you never wear dresses. You've always worn trousers and baggy tops ever since we first met you.'

'I'm going to have to next year. And not just me.' They both looked blankly at her. 'You both need dresses, too,' she added.

'Why?' Holly asked.

'Well, I assume you *will* be my bridesmaids?'

They stared at her, mouths open—then they whooped, hugged her and Judith burst into tears.

'You're really getting married to Brad?' Judith asked. Zoe nodded.

'What took you so long?' Holly teased.

'It couldn't happen to a nicer couple.' Judith mopped her eyes. 'Hey, Holls, we've got a hen party to plan. And a pamper weekend—I think we should drag Zo off to a spa for a weekend, don't you? We can have a massage and facials and saunas and—'

'Hang on,' Zoe said. 'There's something else I need to tell you.'

'You're pregnant?' Holly guessed, and crowed. 'Yay! Jude, we're going to be bridesmaids *and* godmothers next year!'

'Not yet.' Zoe held up both hands in a 'whoa' gesture. 'I'm not pregnant.' At least, she didn't think she was despite the fact that she'd forgotten to get the morning-after pill. 'But I'm not sure I can do this pamper weekend.'

'Why not?' Judith asked.

'Because…' Zoe took a deep breath, and told them about the accident and her scars—though she judged it wise not to tell them about the student they'd all known.

'Oh, Zoe. Why on earth didn't you tell us before?' Holly asked.

'It's not the sort of thing you say when you meet someone, is it? Hi, I'm Zoe and I've had skin grafts.' Zoe grimaced. 'How *not* to make friends.'

'But what about when you got to know us?' Judith asked. 'Didn't you feel you could trust us?'

'It wasn't that I didn't trust you. Of course I do. I'd trust you with my life.' Zoe squeezed her hand. 'It's just that I'd kept the secret for so long…' She shrugged and shook her head. 'I dunno. I just didn't know how to tell you.'

Was it her imagination, or did Holly look faintly uncomfortable? No, you're just seeing a reflection of your own guilt, she told herself.

'What made you decide to tell us now?' Judith asked.

'Because I told Brad. And you're my best friends—I'd already kept it from you both for way too long.' She smiled. 'So, are you going to help me find the right dress—one that doesn't show off my scars?'

'Definitely,' Holly said warmly.

'I want to keep this quiet for now, though,' Zoe warned.

'Why?' Judith asked.

'It's still very new. I need time to get used to it myself, before we tell the world.'

'Just be happy, Zo,' said Holly. 'That's all we want—isn't it, Jude?'

'Absolutely,' Judith agreed.

Zoe smiled at her best friends. 'Thank you. And I am happy. You're right: he's perfect.'

'And you're perfect for him,' Holly added.

'Scars and all,' Zoe said. 'Yeah. I think so.'

'We *know* so,' Judith said. She raised her mug. 'To Zo and Brad. And our future godchildren.'

'Zo, Brad and our godchildren,' Holly echoed, clinking her mug against Judith's.

'When your shifts end, you can do that toast properly. In champagne,' a voice said behind them.

Zoe nearly dropped her coffee. 'How long have you been there?'

'Just long enough to hear that toast.' Brad slid into the spare seat at their table. 'Though I think you two should know she hasn't actually agreed to marry me yet.'

Zoe spread her hands. 'I told you, the answer's yes. When you get the proposal right.'

'How hard can it be? Four little words. ''Will you marry me''?' Judith prompted.

'It's not the words. She's being picky about the location,' Brad explained. Zoe coloured instantly, and he smiled. 'It's your own fault. You should have said yes the first time.'

'Location, hmm?' Holly raised an eyebrow. 'We won't ask. But I reckon your perfect location would be Brandham-on-sea, as the sun's setting.'

'Maybe. I'm working on it.' Brad gave Zoe a speculative look.

'The beach. Hmm, that reminds me, Brad,' Judith said with a grin. 'What's this we hear about skimpy red trunks?'

He groaned. 'Zoe, you didn't tell them?'

'We dragged it out of her,' Holly said, patting his hand. 'Don't worry, your secret's safe with us. Provided, that is, you spoil your bride-to-be rotten.'

'No problem.' Brad kissed the tip of Zoe's nose. 'I only came over to say hello before I get a sandwich to go. Some of us have to take their lunch-breaks at their desks and write reports.'

Judith mimed playing a violin. 'It's so tough, being a consultant,' she said.

'Paperwork and more paperwork. Wait till it's your turn.' He pulled a face back. 'Catch you later.'

'Definitely. We're holding you to that champagne,' Holly said with a smile. 'It isn't every day you get to toast your best friend's engagement!'

CHAPTER THIRTEEN

THE following week, Zoe discovered that she wasn't pregnant. She was shocked to realise that she was disappointed, though she didn't have time to dwell on it. As always, in the winter months, the paediatric ward was snowed under with cases of tiny children battling viruses, on top of their usual heavy workload.

On Christmas Eve, at the end of the early shift, the ward staff gathered in Brad's office. 'I ought to be wearing a Santa outfit to do this properly,' he said. 'But in its absence…' He put on a deep voice. 'Ho, ho, ho. Merry Christmas, all.' He drew the first present out. 'June—this one's for you.'

The staff nurse took her present with a smile. 'Thanks, Santa.'

'Um, aren't you supposed to open it?' he asked in dismay. Unless the presents were opened there and then, this wasn't going to work! Why had he just made assumptions instead of asking Erin?

'Sure, if that's what you want.'

'Yes. It makes it more Christmassy for those of us who are on duty tomorrow,' he said.

June unwrapped her box of chocolates. 'Gorgeous. Thank you, whoever picked my name out!'

More presents followed—the usual bran-tub mix of toiletries and mugs with ribald slogans. There was also a pair of very skimpy red trunks for Brad, bearing the legend SURFBOY written in marker pen across the back.

He groaned. 'I should have expected this, shouldn't I?'

'You're supposed to model them for us,' one of the auxiliaries said, laughing.

'The only surfing I'm doing round here is on the computer,' he teased back.

And finally it was Zoe's turn. With a smile, Brad handed the package to her. 'Merry Christmas, Dr Kennedy.'

Zoe removed the wrapping paper, to discover another layer. And another. And another. With every layer she uncovered, the murmuring and laughter in the room grew louder. And finally she came to a brown envelope. It, in turn, contained a small velvet-covered box.

She swallowed hard. Was this what she thought it was?

'Open it,' Brad said softly.

She did, and the diamond solitaire sparkled in the light. Everyone hushed.

Brad dropped to one knee. 'Will you marry me, Zoe Kennedy?' he asked.

The perfect place. On Christmas Eve, in the middle of the bran-tub draw, with the ward staff around them. Her mouth opened, but the words wouldn't come out.

Tanya, their house officer, nudged her. 'Answer the poor man, Zo!'

Still she couldn't say it, she was beaming too much. So she opened her arms and nodded. Brad picked her up, whirled her round and kissed her, to a round of applause and cheering from their colleagues. Then he took the ring from the box, lifted her left hand and slid the solitaire onto her ring finger.

It fitted perfectly.

Just as she'd known it would.

'Fin's got champagne on ice behind the bar,' Brad said when he finally set her on her feet again. 'And I've got sparkling non-alcoholic stuff for those of you on lates and the night staff.'

It took for ever to leave Brad's office. Everyone in the room wanted to hug them both and kiss them and wish them all the best for the future, and admire the ring that sparkled on Zoe's left hand. Holly and Judith were right in the middle, Zoe noticed. Obviously Brad had told them of his plans and sworn them to secrecy.

After the champagne, someone suggested going to a club, and Brad revealed another talent: he could dance. Really dance. And when he talked the DJ into playing a tango, the floor cleared.

'I can't do this,' Zoe croaked. 'Didn't Jude tell you? I'm really, really not musical. It's not just a tin ear. I've got two left feet as well.'

'Just relax, and follow my lead,' Brad said.

She did, and discovered that it was like dancing on a cloud. Easy. And very, very sexy. At the end, Brad bent her right back over his arm and kissed her, to applause from the onlookers.

'I think,' he said softly, 'the rest of this celebration might be better in private.'

'They'll never let us leave,' Zoe warned, 'even though we're both on early shift tomorrow. I think they're planning to party until the club shuts, and then some.'

'We'll sneak out,' Brad whispered in her ear.

Zoe was still floating on air the next morning. Brad had a half-day and had volunteered to cook the turkey while she finished her rounds. She returned to the smell of roasting turkey with all the trimmings, and a beautifully set dining-room table.

'Wow. I wasn't expecting this.'

'I learned to cook when I was a student,' Brad said.

'Sit.' He handed her a glass of champagne. 'Merry Christmas, Zo.'

'The first of many. Together,' she said, lifting her glass. He echoed the toast.

'And that means sharing the work. Anything I can do?'

'It's all done. But you're obviously itching to know what I've been up to in the kitchen. So go and check on me.'

She chuckled, and headed for the kitchen. 'Chipolatas, bacon rolls, home-made stuffing... I must say, this is a great improvement on my usual Christmas dinner.' She pulled a face at the memory. 'Soggy sprouts in the canteen.'

'Do you normally work over Christmas?' Brad asked.

She nodded. 'I was single and I felt it only fair to let those with families have time off to spend with them.'

'What about your family?' he asked.

'They understand that I'm a doctor, so I don't work sociable hours.'

He tipped his head to one side. 'Have you spent a single Christmas with them since Dermot died?'

'No,' she said quietly.

'Then don't you think it's time to stop punishing them?'

She frowned. 'How do you mean?'

'You said yourself, everyone judged Dermot on the way he looked—that and his bike. And after the accident maybe they were so scared at realising how easily they could have lost you, they didn't really think about what they were saying or what you needed to hear. You know, like when a toddler runs out into the road after a ball, narrowly misses being hit by a car and the mum's so relieved that she goes ballistic and yells at him about road sense instead of hugging him and telling him how much she loves him, even though she *does* love him.' He held her close.

'I never thought of it like that,' she admitted.

'Don't wait until our kids are teenagers and you judge their boyfriends or girlfriends and find them wanting, just like your parents did for you. Go and ring them, honey,' he said softly. 'Wish them happy Christmas while I carve the turkey.'

A few minutes later, Zoe walked back into the kitchen, red-eyed.

'Zo?' He dropped the carving knife and enfolded her in his arms.

'My mum,' Zoe scrubbed at the tears. 'I told her about you. And she started crying. She said all she'd ever wanted was to see me happy. That after Dermot died, she didn't know how to get through to me. She let Jay whisk me away out of sheer desperation, in the hope that someone could help me where she'd failed. And she didn't know how to say how much she loved me and missed me, because I was always the one in the family who was clever with words.'

'Boggle solitaire champ.'

She nodded and sniffed. 'I always felt my parents never understood me. I knew they were proud of me, but sometimes I felt as if I'd stepped from another planet straight into my family's life. I wasn't part of them—except maybe for Jay, and she's everyone's idea of an eccentric aunt.' Her voice cracked. 'But all along, I *was* part of them. I just never knew it.'

'Hey. It's OK.'

'She wants to meet you. So does Dad.'

'Whenever you're ready,' Brad promised.

It was the best Christmas Zoe could ever remember. She called in enough favours so her off-duty shifts after

Christmas matched Brad's, and just before New Year a tearful reunion with her parents—who took to Brad immediately and welcomed him to the family—was followed by the drive north to Norfolk.

On the last day of the year, Brad woke her with a cup of coffee and fresh croissants from the local bakery. 'We're playing tourists today,' he informed her.

'Where?'

'Wait and see.' Clearly her doubts must have shown on her face, because he smiled. 'It doesn't involve a motorbike. Promise. But I'm driving and you're not to look at any signposts.'

'Brad, I spent a year living here. I don't need signposts to know where I am.'

'Hmm. Maybe I'd better blindfold you,' he teased.

Teasing led to tickling, tickling led to kissing, kissing led to making love, and it was almost lunch-time before Brad drove them away from Marsh End.

As soon as they reached their destination, Zoe squeaked. 'Hunstanton. We're going fossil-hunting?'

'So much for me trying to surprise you,' he said ruefully.

'Well, of course I'd recognise it! It's the only place in Norfolk with stripy cliffs like that.'

'And, according to the websites I was checking out, it's the best place around here to find fossils.'

'I wouldn't put it past you to have bought one from the rock shop in Brandham,' Zoe said, 'and then hide it on the beach so I "discover" it.'

'I did consider it,' he admitted. 'But I figured you'd guess what I'd done.'

They spent the afternoon beachcombing, poking around the rocks. And then Zoe dropped to her knees. 'You're absolutely sure you didn't go to the rock shop?' she asked.

'Cross my heart.' Brad performed the little gesture. 'Why?'

She held a small rock up to show him. 'Look. I've actually found a fossil. My own fossil,' she breathed.

He kissed her. 'Congratulations.'

'Here.' She gave it to him.

He examined it closely. 'I don't know what it is, but it's impressive.' He handed it back to her.

She shook her head. 'It's yours.'

'But it's the first one you've ever found.'

'Like Christmas. The first of many together,' she said softly. 'And I want you to have it.'

Brad slid the little rock into his pocket and kissed her again. 'Thank you.'

Later that afternoon they walked along the beach at Brandham and watched the sun set.

'No surfers this time,' Brad said. 'And this was how I wanted to walk with you before.'

'Me, too. Except I was too scared.'

'Are you scared any more?' he asked.

'Not when you're with me.'

'Good.' He tightened his arm round her.

'Look, there's the wishing star.' She pointed up to the sky. 'You asked Lara to marry you under the wishing star.'

'And now she's at peace. I've learned to let her go,' Brad said softly. 'Maybe that's Lara looking down on us now, telling us to be happy.' He kissed her gently. 'We're lucky, you know. Some people don't even have this once. And you and I have been granted it twice.'

'First with Lara and Dermot, and now with each other.'

'Yeah. Lucky beyond belief.'

She nodded. 'I can't remember ever being this happy.'

'Believe it. Because it's only going to get better,' Brad promised.

They stayed up to see in the new year—watching the village fireworks out of the window—and the next day it was time to return to London. They stopped by Brad's flat to pick up some clothes, and there was a pile of post on the doormat.

'Junk mail, junk mail, bank statement—hmm.' Brad opened the letter, scanned it swiftly, and handed it to Zoe without a word.

She read it. 'It's from the trust. They're offering you a permanent post. Paediatric consultant at London City General.'

'Yep.'

'What are you going to do?'

He spread his hands. 'It all depends where you want to live after we get married.'

'I hadn't really thought about it,' she said honestly.

'You could come back to the States with me. Or I could stay here with you. It doesn't matter, as long as we're together.'

She frowned. 'What about your family? Won't they want you to go home?'

Brad shrugged. 'Probably not.'

'But...'

'They're not like your family, Zo. We're not close. We didn't even live in the same state. So they wouldn't see any more of me if we go to the States than they would if I stayed here.'

'Do they know about me?'

He nodded. 'I rang and told them a while back.' His mother had made a vague comment and started talking about herself, and his brother had half-heartedly congratulated him and made some excuse that he was on his way out to the gym, so he couldn't stop to chat.

At the time, it hadn't bothered Brad. But the reaction of Zoe's family had made him realise just what he was missing. Her parents had sent flowers. Her aunts, uncles and cousins had all sent cards to congratulate them. Jay had sent a bottle of vintage champagne from France. Whereas his mother and brother were relying on the fact that they were 'too far away' to make any sort of gesture.

'Are they coming to the wedding?'

'Probably not,' Brad said. He hadn't bothered asking them because he knew there would be some excuse why they couldn't make it. That, or his mother would make sure she was the centre of attention on Zoe's special day. He didn't want to risk that. 'It's a long way to come for one day. And, as I said, we're not close.' At her dismayed look, he kissed the tip of her nose. 'Leave it, Zo. It stopped worrying me a long, long time ago. And, talking of the wedding, we haven't set a date. Or decided where we're going to live.' He smiled. 'We have a choice. Hospital flat or your house.'

'Don't you want somewhere bigger?'

He shook his head. 'I love your house.'

'My place it is, then.' Zoe paused. 'We don't have to wait until we get married. Unless you're being ultra-traditional.'

'Move in with you, you mean?'

'If you want to.'

He nuzzled her cheek. 'Oh, I do.'

'That's settled, then. I'll help you pack.'

'There's no rush,' he said. 'I've got to give notice to the trust anyway.'

'We could move your stuff on our next day off,' she suggested.

He nodded. 'Sounds good to me. But, right now, all I want is a long, hot bath. And bed.' He drew his thumb along her lower lip. 'Both of them shared with you.'

Four days later, they both had a half-day. Brad claimed they could pack and move his things in an afternoon, because he hadn't brought much over to England.

'What about your things in America?' she asked.

'They're in storage. I'll give the furniture to charity—my old neighbour used to run a support group for battered wives—and most of the paperwork can be junked.'

'Don't you need to go and sort them out?'

He shook his head. 'The storage place will do it for me.'

'But things like photographs?' she persisted.

He shrugged. 'There's plenty of time. Later.'

Brad packed his clothes while Zoe packed the contents of his living-room shelves into sturdy cardboard boxes. Most of the books were textbooks on paediatrics, but there was a leather-bound book of poetry. When she picked it up, a photograph fell out.

A photograph of an extremely beautiful woman.

Lara.

She was wearing a shoulderless black sheath dress, with a wrap loosely draped round her shoulders. Her long blonde hair was twisted up into a sophisticated knot, and she was laughing.

And she was everything that Zoe wasn't. Tall, rail-thin, effortlessly glamorous. And unscarred.

Brad had said Zoe was glamorous enough for him. How *could* she be, when he'd been married to someone this beautiful?

She knew she shouldn't do it, but she couldn't resist turning the photograph over. And there, in neat script—a million miles away from Zoe's doctory scrawl—was a message. *Brad. Love you for ever. Lara. Xx*

Zoe swallowed the threatening tears, making her throat ache. *For ever.* She had no doubt that Lara had had a similar photograph of Brad in formal dress—a dinner jacket and cummerbund—with a similar inscription on the back.

For ever.

Even though Brad had said it was time to move on, that he wanted to make a new life with her—even though she'd thought they were happy—doubts rushed up to swamp her. It had all happened so quickly—from meeting Brad to making love to telling him about the accident and then agreeing to marry him. And now they were moving in together.

Maybe it was too fast. Too soon. Maybe they were rushing into it without really thinking it through. Maybe Brad had wanted her because he was lonely, and she was so different from Lara that she wouldn't remind him of his late wife. Maybe she should call a halt right now. Give them some space and time to see what they *really* wanted.

'Zo? How's it going?'

Guiltily, she slipped the photograph back into the poetry book and tucked it into the box with his textbooks. 'Fine. Just wool-gathering.'

'Flicking through my textbooks, more like,' he teased. 'I know what you're like. You've even got a paediatric encyclopaedia next to your bed!'

'It's a fair cop, guv,' she said, putting her hands up in mock surrender. Her face felt hot and she only hoped Brad would put it down to his teasing, not the fact that he'd so nearly caught her prying.

'Here. Coffee-break,' he said, handing her a mug.

'Cheers.' She forced herself to smile at him. She loved

him—but she really wasn't sure any more that they were doing the right thing. Somehow, she had to find the words to explain. To slow things down. Give them time.

Or maybe it would be all right when he was sharing her home properly, when he'd moved in and they'd got used to each other. Maybe she was just worrying over nothing.

But the doubts still gnawed away at her, to the point where she spent much of that night awake, listening to Brad's regular breathing and wondering how she was going to sort things out without hurting him. She loved him, she was sure of that, but was this too soon for Brad? Would he wake up one day and realise he'd made a huge mistake—that he really wanted another Lara?

Somehow, she had to find a way of asking him. But tact wasn't her strong point. And if she asked him straight, it could splinter the trust that had built between them, to the point where everything would collapse beyond the point of repair.

What on earth was she going to do?

CHAPTER FOURTEEN

WHILE she was working out how to approach Brad, Zoe buried herself in work. 'No rush, you said,' she said, when Brad brought up the subject of their wedding. 'We're fine as we are for now.'

Except it wasn't fine. Her doubts grew with each passing day, and it started to affect her work—to the point where she found herself talking to worried parents in medicalese instead of trying to explain things clearly to them, the way she usually did. As soon as she'd examined nine-month-old Jacob Walters she said, 'Indirect inguinal hernia.' When she saw the blank looks on his parents' faces, she knew she'd done the one thing she'd always promised herself she'd never do.

'Sorry. Ignore the jargon. What that really means is that part of his intestines have pushed through a weakness or tear in the wall of his abdomen into his groin. And that's what this bulge is here, in his scrotum.' She pointed to the smooth mass. 'You'll probably find it's bigger when he's been crying, because that puts strain on the abdominal wall, and it'll be smaller after he's had a sleep when he's been relaxing.'

'Our health visitor noticed it the last time I had him weighed,' Sharon Walters said. 'Jacob hates having his clothes taken off, so he made a fuss. Then she saw the bulge and said we needed to have it checked out properly.'

'It's very common and it's treatable,' Zoe reassured them. 'It doesn't hurt him at all, even though it looks uncomfortable. It's on the right-hand side—again, that's twice as common as the left side—and it's not a case of an undescended testicle or a testicle that goes back, what we term "retractile".' She palpated both testes. 'There's something we call a "silk sign"—when I feel the hernia sac over the cord of his testicle, it feels as if I'm rubbing two layers of silk together. So that's pretty definite—it's a hernia.'

'What happens now?' Kirk Walters asked.

'I'll need to book him in for surgery. It's not an emergency operation, but I want to avoid a situation where too much of the intestine goes through the gap in the muscle. If that happens and the muscle squeezes, it'll cut off the blood supply to the intestine, and he'll be in a lot of pain.' As well as potentially causing a lot of damage to the intestine.

'But he's only little. Isn't surgery…well, dangerous?' Sharon asked.

'No, it's fine. It'll be a day procedure so he can go home afterwards. Children under five recover really quickly, so he can go back to his normal activities forty-eight hours after surgery. I'll prescribe pain relief for the first forty-eight hours, and you'll see bruising and swelling in his scrotum for up to three weeks, but he'll be fine.' She smiled at them. 'Let's go and book him in. I've got some leaflets that can tell you a bit more about hernias, but feel free to ring me if you've got any questions.'

Brad caught her on the way back from booking her patient in for surgery. 'Hey. I haven't seen much of you lately.'

'We've been working different shifts. You know what it's like, being a medic,' she prevaricated.

'Got two minutes for a chat in my office?'

She shook her head. 'Sorry. I'm a bit pushed for time.'

'Please, Zo.'

She couldn't resist that smile, the little-boy-lost look. 'All right. Two minutes—but that's *only* two minutes,' she warned.

Brad closed the door behind them. 'Zo, I know this is the wrong time and the wrong place to ask you…but I know that something's wrong. What is it?'

'Nothing,' she lied.

He shook his head. 'You've gone distant on me pretty much since the day I moved in with you. And you look as if you haven't slept properly in days—for all the wrong reasons. Have you changed your mind about us, honey?'

She sucked in a breath. 'No-o.'

It didn't sound very definite. It sounded really, really weak to her ears. And Brad clearly picked up on it, too, because he raked a hand through his hair and sighed. 'Zo, something's up. If I've done something or said something to upset you, then tell me. Please. So I can put it right.'

'You haven't done anything.' She sighed. 'It's just…'

'What?'

'There isn't an easy way to say this,' she said.

'Then give it to me straight.'

'I don't want to hurt you.'

'You'll hurt me more by not telling me.'

She dug her fingers into her palms. 'This whole thing…it's all happening too fast,' she said. 'We hardly know each other, yet we're planning the rest of our lives together.'

'You already know everything about me. I'm the younger of two boys, I grew up in California, I worked as a lifeguard while I was at college. I trained as a paediatrician. I was married before but my wife and baby died. I came here on secondment and I met you. I love you. What else do you need to know?'

Zoe shook her head. 'It's all happening too fast,' she said again. 'And I'm as opposite from Lara as you can get. Hair, height, body, eyes, the lot. You said yourself she was quiet and a little shy, whereas I'm noisy and bustling. What if I'm your transition person, Brad? What if you only *think* you love me—and then, after we're married, you meet someone who's more in tune with you?'

'That's not going to happen, Zo. I love you.' His eyes were very blue, very earnest. 'Yes, I fell for you fast and I fell for you hard—but that doesn't make how I feel any less valid.' He paused. 'How do you feel about me?'

The question she'd been dreading. 'Right now, I don't know,' she whispered. 'I love you. Or am I just grateful because you're the one who's finally got me to come to terms with my scars? I don't know. It's as if I'm on some kind of a fairground ride, Brad, and I'm going faster and faster, round and round and round, and I'm not sure I can handle this.' She bit her lip. 'It's not you. It's me. I'm scared that we're not giving ourselves enough time to be sure we're doing the right thing.' And more: she was scared that she wouldn't live up to Lara. That Brad would discover he'd settled for a very poor substitute.

'Maybe you're right. Maybe we need to slow things down a little.' He looked at her. 'I've still got the lease of the flat. Do you want me to move my stuff back?'

'I don't know.' She rubbed her hand across her eyes. 'In some ways, yes, in others, no.'

'You need time. I'll move out, give you some space, until you're sure of what you want,' Brad said. 'You're on a late and I'm on an early, so I'll make sure my stuff's shifted before you get home.' His smile was bleak. 'Maybe we can see each other some time this week. Spend a while getting to know each other.'

'Yeah.' Zoe twisted her engagement ring round on her

finger. 'Maybe…maybe I should give…' The rest of the words stuck in her throat. How could she continue wearing his ring after this? Silently, she pulled the ring from her finger and handed it to him.

For a long, long moment, he was silent. Then he shrugged. 'OK, if that's what you want. I'll leave it to you, Zo. Call me when you want to see me.'

She nodded, too choked to speak, and left his office.

At the end of her shift, Zoe couldn't face going home. She rang Holly, who clearly heard the misery in her voice and demanded that Zoe come straight round: she and Jude would be waiting with ice-cream and lattes.

As soon as Zoe was seated on the sofa, tub of premium ice-cream and spoon in hand, they persuaded her to spill the beans.

Holly stared at her in shock. 'You did *what*?'

'I didn't set out with the intention of giving him back his ring. I just wanted to slow things down a little.' Zoe ate another spoonful of ice-cream straight from the tub.

'There's slowing down, and there's stopping things right in their tracks. I thought you loved him?' Holly said.

'I did. I *do*. I just wanted to get off the roller-coaster.'

'There's more to it than that,' Judith said quietly. 'You don't do doubts, Zo. What happened?'

Zoe shook her head. 'It's crazy.'

'No crazier than breaking off your engagement to the man you love—and who loves you. And he really does love you, Zo. It's clear to anyone who sees you together,' Holly said. 'So what's the real problem?'

Zoe sighed. 'All right. I saw a picture of Lara.'

'And?' Judith prompted.

'And she was everything that I'm not. Then I started

thinking. What if Brad chose me deliberately because I'm her opposite?'

'Have you asked him that?' Holly asked.

'Yes.'

'And?'

Zoe sighed. 'He said it wasn't like that. And he loves me.'

'Do you love him?' Judith asked.

'Yes, but that's not the point. Supposing I'm not what he really wants? He thinks he wants me now, but it's all happened so fast. Am I just for now, or for always? And how do I know which it is?'

'Sounds to me,' Holly said softly, 'like a case of pre-wedding panic. You've got the jitters, Zo.'

'So he's moving out today?' Judith asked.

'Yes. And it's going to be weird without him,' Zoe admitted. 'But a divorce six months down the line would be much worse.'

'I think you two just need to talk. Spend some time together. You might find that he's panicking, too,' Holly said.

'He might be worried that he won't live up to Dermot's memory,' Judith pointed out.

'That's different. Dermot was a long, long time ago. Nearly half my life,' Zoe protested. 'Lara was much more recent.'

'It doesn't mean Brad can't love you just as much as he loved her,' Holly said. 'You're different people and he probably loves different things about you. Does that make him less sincere?'

'I don't know,' Zoe said.

Judith hugged her. 'Look, whatever you decide in the end, we're here for you. Whether we're going to take you dress shopping to find something to stun your bridegroom, or whether we cheer you up by a tour of every ice-cream bar in London—we're here.'

'Thanks.' Zoe gave her best friends a watery smile. 'I know I'm probably being stupid.'

'But you're scared.' Judith squeezed her hand. 'You need to take a step back. Talk about it. Until you're both sure you're doing the right thing.'

'There's one question you need to be able to answer,' Holly said, surprising Zoe. 'If you never, ever saw him again—how would you feel? No, don't answer now.' She held her hand up to forestall Zoe's answer. 'Just think about it. And when you know the answer, you'll know what to do.'

When Zoe finally went home, her house felt empty and her bed felt far too wide. Not to mention cold. Zoe was shocked at how quickly she'd grown used to Brad's body heat curled round her at night. At three in the morning, she was tempted to ring him and tell him she'd made a mistake, that she wanted him. But he was probably asleep, and it wouldn't be fair. Right now she missed him, but the doubts were still there. And they'd still be there in the morning.

As for Holly's question: she felt too drained, too miserable to answer it. Everything had suddenly gone wrong and slid down an abyss, and she wasn't sure why or how, or even how to drag herself out of it.

Tomorrow, she promised herself.

Except Brad was busy all day, and barely did more than nod an acknowledgement to her on the ward. Before she realised it, he'd left for the day. The next few days were more of the same, and she remembered what he'd said to her. *Call me when you want to see me.*

So she did. His mobile phone rang once, twice, then

she heard the message she'd hoped to avoid. 'This is the voicemail service for—'

She cut the connection before the recorded message gave Brad's number. She could leave it until tomorrow. Or… She rummaged in her handbag for her mobile phone, then sent him a text. *Dinner 2moro? Z.*

She left the phone on, waiting for a reply. It felt like more than just an hour before her phone beeped. *Where & when? Am on lates. B.*

Not Giovanni's. Somewhere that didn't hold memories for either of them. She named a pizza parlour on the other side of the hospital and suggested 9.30 p.m.

A few seconds later, her phone beeped again. *OK.*

OK? Was that it? Then she smiled at her own outrage. Brad was giving her space. Even if he'd wanted to send her a message of love, he'd have worried that maybe she'd feel he was pushing her too hard. OK was just that— neutral, wary, waiting for her move.

Brad was late. Zoe had already drunk a glass of red wine by the time he turned up.

'Sorry. I had a patient with an acute asthma attack. The dad decided that the petting farm would be a good place to take his daughter for the day. He's not on good terms with the mum, so he didn't bother listening to her about the inhalers. Delivered her home, and then she started wheezing badly.' He rolled his eyes. 'She's stable now, but I'll need to have a chat with the dad and explain to him that there's sometimes a delayed reaction to an asthma trigger. Maybe he'll listen to me where he won't accept it from the mum.'

'Pet dander?' Zoe said, pouring him a glass of wine.

'Probably.' Brad took a sip of his wine. 'Thanks.

Anyway, how are you?' He added softly, 'You look like hell.'

'I feel it,' she admitted.

'Have you come to a decision?'

She shook her head. 'I'm miserable without you. But I'm scared. About us.'

'What can I do to stop you being scared?'

'I don't know.'

The waiter saved her from answering any more questions. They both ordered a Napoletana pizza with a salad to share. Then Brad looked at her, his face utterly unreadable. 'So. Where do we go from here?'

'I don't know.' She remembered Holly's question. 'If you never, ever saw me again, how would you feel?'

Brad went very, very still. Then he sucked in a breath as if she'd punched him in the stomach. 'Are you telling me you don't want to see me again?'

'No, I'm just asking. How would you feel?'

He was silent for a long, long time. 'As if the sun had stopped shining.' He raised an eyebrow. 'And you?'

'I…' She fought for breath. 'Right now, I feel frozen inside. I can't answer that.'

He leaned his elbows on the table and steepled his hands. 'Zo, we can't go on like this. I've tried to be patient, I really have, but I can't take any more. You're going to have to make a decision.'

'I can't.'

'Can't, or won't?'

She didn't answer.

'If you won't, I will. Maybe we'd better end it before either of us gets any more hurt. Goodbye, Zoe.' He stood up. 'I'll settle the bill.'

'But you haven't eaten.'

'Doesn't matter. I'm not hungry any more.'

She knew she should stop him going. Right now. But she couldn't move. It was as if someone had petrified her and she was made of frozen marble. So all she could do was watch him as he walked out of her life.

Brad woke next morning feeling hung-over. More from lack of sleep than too much to drink. He'd had half a glass of red wine with Zoe last night, and no more.

Zoe. No more. The words echoed in his head.

Oh, hell.

A tepid shower didn't make him feel any better. But at least he knew she had two days off. Two days when maybe she'd have time to think, time to change her mind. He forced himself to concentrate on work, but with every minute the tension coiled tighter inside him. When would she call?

When she was due back on the ward, Brad was on leave. The first day, he sat by the phone. She'd call him. She had to.

The second day, he realised that she wasn't going to call.

Working with her after this wasn't an option. Although he'd grown to feel that London City General was home, he couldn't stay here. Couldn't watch Zoe fall in love with someone else. So there was only one thing he could do.

With a heavy heart he made a phone call. Then he texted Zoe to ask her to dinner that evening after her shift. It was feeble and pathetic and weak—he knew all that—but he couldn't face talking to her. Just in case she said no.

It seemed like for ever before his mobile phone bleeped, telling him that he had a message. Let it be her. Please, let it be her.

It was. And it was a yes. A polite, cool little OK. But
that was fine. At least he'd have the chance to say goodbye properly.

Adrenaline tingled at the ends of Zoe's fingers. She was
almost—almost—tempted to just walk away again. But
she'd already hurt Brad enough. The least she could do
was have dinner with him and listen to whatever it was
he had to say.

She rang the doorbell, and the tingling spread to the
back of her neck with every passing second.

He opened the door. 'Hi. Come in.'

'I, um, brought you this.' She handed him the bottle of
wine.

'Thank you.' He ushered her into the flat.

Zoe's eyes narrowed. Although the table was laid beautifully—including vanilla-scented candles—the shelves
were completely bare. Clearly he hadn't unpacked since
moving from her place. Why? Had he been too miserable
to bother, or was he expecting her to change her mind
tonight?

She picked at the tiger prawns and pawpaw Brad put
before her. And then she gave up. 'Brad, why did you ask
me over tonight?'

'To apologise—for rushing you.'

Then she looked properly at him and realised what
she'd missed. The sombre look in his eyes. 'You haven't
unpacked.'

'No. That's the other reason I asked you over. So I
could say goodbye.'

'Goodbye?'

'I'm going back to the States.'

'But…why?'

'London City General is your patch. I can start again

somewhere else.' He lifted one shoulder. 'I wish things could have been different.'

'You're leaving because of me?'

'It's not fair to either of us as it is.' He raked a hand through his hair. 'I'm slowly going out of my mind, seeing you and knowing I can't have you. I don't want us to end up hating each other.'

Zoe frowned. 'I don't hate you, Brad. Not at all.'

'But you don't love me. I knew you had doubts, but I thought I could love you enough for both of us. I was wrong. I put too much pressure on you. So I'd rather you were free to find someone you can love.' He twisted his wineglass between his fingers. 'I didn't want to just sneak away without telling you. They're getting a locum in.' He smiled ruefully. 'A locum for a locum. So I'll be out of your life after tonight.'

Out of her life? Zoe sank back into her chair as if someone had pushed her. Hard.

'Be happy, Zoe. I hope you find someone who deserves you.'

'But…' No. This was all wrong.

Holly's question echoed in her mind. *If you never, ever saw him again—how would you feel?*

Then it hadn't meant anything. Now she was facing the reality. If she let him go now, she was never going to see him again. 'Like I've fallen over the edge of a precipice, with a patch of sun and sky growing smaller and smaller and smaller with every second.'

'What?' Brad stared at her, frowning.

'If you go. That's what it'd be like.' She reached across the table and took his hand. 'Don't go.'

'I can't stay. I love you, Zoe, and I want you to be happy—but I can't stay and watch you fall in love with someone else. Don't ask me.' His voice was cracked, as if she'd pinned him to a rack and turned the handle too many times.

'I'm not going to fall in love with anyone else. How could I, when I love you? Look, I know I've been amazingly stupid, but will you give me a second chance?'

Hope flickered in his eyes. 'You mean that?'

She nodded. 'I love you, Brad. I was just scared…scared I couldn't match up to Lara, scared that this was all too soon and you'd wake up one morning and realise you'd made a mistake.'

'I made a mistake all right,' he said softly. 'I rushed you because I wanted you so much. I didn't want to have to wait for the rest of my life.' His fingers tightened round hers. 'But don't worry about Lara. You're not her. I know that and I don't want you even to try to be Lara. Yes, I loved her and part of me always will, but I want to spend the rest of my life with you. And, yes, it's happened fast, but that doesn't make it any the less real.'

'I've made such a mess of this.'

'You and me both.'

'Brad—' Zoe's words were cut off by a high-pitched shriek.

'Smoke detector!' Brad said, and raced into the kitchen. He pulled the chicken breasts from under the grill, dumped the charred remains in the sink and ran cold water over them, then frantically flapped a tea-towel underneath the smoke detector.

When the noise finally stopped, he looked over to the doorway to see Zoe there. She was crying.

'Zo? I'm sorry. I'm so sorry.' He held her close. She was shaking. 'Please, don't cry.'

She mumbled something he couldn't catch.

He let her go for long enough to look into her eyes and wipe away the tears. 'What?'

'I'm not crying,' she said, clutching her stomach.

Then he realised, and rolled his eyes. 'I don't think I'm ever going to understand the English sense of humour.'

'You've got a lifetime to learn. If...' Zoe sobered. 'If you want to.'

'Oh, I do.' He kissed her. 'Starting now.'

'Mmm. While I still have some sense left, you've got a phone call to make. Cancelling your resignation and advising a change of address.'

'Are you sure about this?' Brad asked. 'I'm not going to rush you again.'

She stood on tiptoe and pulled his head down to hers. 'I'm sure.'

EPILOGUE

Two months later.

'DO I REALLY look all right?' Zoe asked.

Holly and Judith groaned in tandem. 'You look like a princess,' Holly said. 'We told you that when we went dress shopping.'

Zoe was wearing a simple raw silk dress with a boat-shaped neck and long sleeves that hid her scars. Her veil, too, was very simple, and she carried a hand-tied bouquet of white roses.

'Brad will fall to his knees when he sees you,' Judith predicted. 'All the women will weep, and all the men will think about standing up and objecting, then absconding with you.'

Zoe grinned. 'Don't over-egg it, Jude.'

'Come on. You can't be traditionally late today,' Holly said. 'I don't think Brad could handle it.'

'No. I was a complete cow to him.'

'You had doubts. Better to wait until you were sure,' Judith said. 'Come on. I'll tell your dad you're ready.'

Ten minutes later, the wedding cars pulled up outside the church. Holly and Judith, both in pale aquamarine dresses, alighted first, and then Zoe's father helped her out of the car.

'Ready, love?' he asked, squeezing her arm.

'Ready,' she whispered.

As the first notes of Purcell's Trumpet Voluntary sounded, Zoe took a deep breath and walked down the aisle. Her family filled one side of the church; their friends filled the other. And Brad stood by the altar, waiting for her with a smile of such love and brilliance, Zoe's heart melted.

This was where they'd both heal their scars at last.

As they stood before the rector, Zoe looked at Brad.

'You can back out now, if you want to,' he whispered. There was a flash of panic in his eyes—panic Zoe realised he was trying to conceal, for her sake. Because Brad loved her enough to let her go, if this wasn't right for her, too.

She smiled. 'No chance,' she said softly. 'This is for now, for always. I love you.'

As she took his hand, the rector spoke. 'Dearly beloved, we are gathered here…'

MILLS & BOON

A very special

Mother's Day

Margaret Way
Anne Herries

Indulge all of your romantic senses with these two brand-new stories.

On sale 4th March 2005

Available at most branches of WHSmith, Tesco, ASDA, Martins, Borders, Eason, Sainsbury's and all good paperback bookshops.

4 FREE

BOOKS AND A SURPRISE GIFT!

We would like to take this opportunity to thank you for reading this Mills & Boon® book by offering you the chance to take FOUR more specially selected titles from the Medical Romance™ series absolutely FREE! We're also making this offer to introduce you to the benefits of the Reader Service™—

- ★ FREE home delivery
- ★ FREE gifts and competitions
- ★ FREE monthly Newsletter
- ★ Exclusive Reader Service offers
- ★ Books available before they're in the shops

Accepting these FREE books and gift places you under no obligation to buy, you may cancel at any time, even after receiving your free shipment. Simply complete your details below and return the entire page to the address below. You don't even need a stamp!

YES! Please send me 4 free Medical Romance books and a surprise gift. I understand that unless you hear from me, I will receive 6 superb new titles every month for just £2.69 each, postage and packing free. I am under no obligation to purchase any books and may cancel my subscription at any time. The free books and gift will be mine to keep in any case.

M5ZED

Ms/Mrs/Miss/Mr ....Initials ....

BLOCK CAPITALS PLEASE

Surname ....

Address ....

....

....Postcode..

Send this whole page to:
UK: FREEPOST CN81, Croydon, CR9 3WZ